"Looks like murder one," Dino announced grimly. "The guys found the back of her skull caved in. Unless the medical examiner finds water in her lungs, which at this point I doubt, my guess is that May Minton was bludgeoned to death. You called it again, honey."

A cold tremor swept over Nina. "I can't say that I'm exactly filled with pride." Her voice broke. "God, what am I—some kind of lightning rod for murder and mayhem?"

Rossi's voice was deep and comforting. "This kind of crap happens. Don't go blaming yourself." He sighed. "Hide-and-seek time again."

Nina fought back tears. "Oh, Dino, who'd murder such a wonderful woman? What did she ever do to deserve it?"

"My thoughts exactly. I figure it's probably connected with this role on *The Turning Seasons*. She's been out of the limelight fifteen years and nobody's bothered her. But the minute she comes out of retirement—no more May Minton."

"It does seem like more than mere coincidence."

"Somebody on the show could have been scared enough to make sure that May Minton never got line one out of her mouth. Any candidates?"

Nina thought. "Yes, it sounds like May's comeback could have something to do with it. But we mustn't go off half-cocked. I'm sure there are possibilities we haven't even thought about yet."

Take One for Murder

Eileen Fulton's
DEATH of a
GOLDEN GIRL

IVY BOOKS • NEW YORK

Grateful acknowledgment is made
to Mr. Thomas P. Ramirez
for his editorial advice and counsel.

Ivy Books
Published by Ballantine Books
Copyright © 1988 by Butterfield Press, Inc. & Eileen Fulton

Produced by Butterfield Press, Inc.
133 Fifth Avenue
New York, New York 10003

Back cover photograph: Tom Gates

Library of Congress Catalog Card Number: 87-91045

ISBN 0-8041-0196-5

Manufactured in the United States of America

First Edition: June 1988

To Merrill Lemmon,
who made this book possible
just by being himself.

Chapter One

It was 10:05 A.M. of a Wednesday morning in early October. While New York City basked in its first tangy, teasing sample of autumn—especially welcome after a long, oppressively muggy and warm summer—inside the Meyer Productions studios on West 66th Street it was chaotic business as usual, the weather electronically controlled, holding at a steady seventy-two degrees, winter or summer.

Sixteen actors were on call that morning; six scenes had to be in the can before 4:00 P.M. Spence Sprague, the director of *The Turning Seasons*, one of television's longest-running and most popular soap operas, had long since finished the full group line rehearsals and had turned the cast over to the assistant directors, Bellamy Carter and Nick Galano. Scene by scene, the two ramrods had shaped up the blocking rehearsals until they were satisfied that the day's episode would proceed with no major glitches.

For the moment the cast was adrift, savoring free time to study scripts and run lines among themselves. Or, as Nina McFall, Robin Tally, and Susan Levy were doing, to recharge batteries and straighten out their revision-muddled heads. There were times when cast members got into their roles

1

so deeply that they ran the danger of losing touch with the real world. When that happened to an actor, he became vulnerable, and risked becoming a candidate for the proverbial rubber room.

The break was indefinite—there was no telling when Galano or Carter would summon individual groups for fine tuning on interpretation, lines, and positions on the sets—so the trio made the best of it, keeping vigil at the main rehearsal room's soda machine while grousing, gossiping, and idle chitchat held sway.

"Bellamy's certainly in a mellow mood today,' said Nina McFall. A fixture of *The Turning Seasons* for five years and firmly established in her role as Melanie Prescott, super office-bitch, Nina was at the peak of her profession as a soap opera star. She was thirty-four, single, and the possessor of a gorgeous figure, perfect teeth, peaches-and-cream complexion, and the most startling head of red hair Mother Nature had ever created. Today the flaming crown looked particularly luscious in contrast to the green outfit she wore. "He just about took my head off when I came in too soon on that boardroom scene."

"Probably had a tiff on the home front," replied Susan Levy, twenty-three, who with her honey-blond hair, pixie face, smoldering eyes, and pouty lips was one of the youngest females in the TTS cast. "So he takes it out on us. You've heard of surrogate wives, haven't you? Well, welcome to the club."

"Come on, Susan," Nina scolded softly, her pretty brows furrowing. "Get off of it, will you? It's how he does his job that matters. He's an excellent director most of the time. So judge not. Sure, he gets unreasonable at times, but don't we all? He knows his stuff; he keeps us on our toes."

"Self-protection, pure and simple," Robin sniped, rolling her eyes mischievously. Abruptly she lost interest in the conversation and began inspecting her nails, dark carmine against an almost unnaturally pale skin. Jet-black hair, worn long and severe, helped to emphasize her stark beauty. One of a half dozen ingenues the show boasted, Robin played the sympathetic role of Buffy Kingston, the tyrannized daughter of Horace Kingston, an industrialist tycoon who rode roughshod over Kingston Falls, the town where most of the TTS action took place. Ironically enough, Horace Kingston was played by Noel Winston, a white-haired grandfather and the cast's most lovable pussycat.

"What do you think about that new twist in your romance with Jett?" Nina now asked Robin, her closest friend on the set. She referred to a plot change where Buffy Kingston's father was now forbidding her to see her ad-man lover, Jett Ransome, and was pushing her instead at Harvey Stone, a fiftyish business confederate whose wife was dying of cancer. "Sounds pretty trashy to me."

Robin pulled a face. "Worse than that, try doing it with Dez Folwell. You been close to him lately? His breath would start a windmill in an oil painting." She sighed. "The sacrifices we make for art."

"And whose bright idea was that, do you suppose?" Susan asked. "The script change, I mean."

"I'll give you three guesses," Robin said, "and you won't need the second two."

"Helen Meyer?"

"Susan," Nina quipped, her green eyes glinting, "you prescient child. Go to the head of the class." Then, more soberly, "It certainly isn't a character twist Dave Gelber would dream up."

"I wonder when that man's going to get backbone enough to tell Helen what she can do with her dippy ideas," Robin said. "I was sure, with Morty gone, that she'd settle back, enjoy life, and leave us alone. God, if I had her money, I'd be on a cruise every other week.''

''But she is easing off somewhat,'' Nina said. ''She even smiled and said hello to me when she came in on Monday. Could it be that she's finally stopped blaming me for what happened to her loathsome stepson?''

''I sure hope so,'' Robin teased. ''Though you certainly were unreasonable. To expect dear Byron to spend the rest of his life in prison, just because he happened to murder three people, including his own father. Nina,'' she winked, ''you can be such a royal pain at times.''

''Have you heard about Helen's latest brainstorm?'' Nina asked, taking a sip from her can of diet soda. ''The 'Golden Girls' clone? Not that I disagree. It's a good idea—possibly the only original thought Helen's had in years.''

Robin frowned. ''The May Minton thing? I've heard some rumors, but nothing definite.''

''Who is this May Minsky, anyway?'' Susan asked. ''Sounds like a burlesque queen.'' Robin simply stared at Susan in pity while Nina choked on the last of her cold drink. ''Did I say something wrong?''

''Nina, will you please put this child out of her misery? Even *I* know who May Minton is.''

''Oh, never mind the wisecracks. Just tell me.''

Although Robin knew the basic headlines about the lady in question, she deferred to Nina because theater history was an area where Nina outshone nearly everyone in the cast, with the exception of Noel Winston, Mary Kennerly, and—occasionally— Angela Dolan.

''Without exaggeration,'' Nina said after a perfectly timed pause, ''May Minton was one of the finest talents ever to grace the American stage or light up what was probably still known at the time as 'the silver screen.' She was a name you mentioned in the same breath with Katherine Cornell, Laurette Taylor, Margaret Sullavan, Lynne Fontanne . . .'' she trailed off, recognizing the mystified glaze on Susan's face, and cut it short. ''She was a big star about thirty years ago.''

''God. She must be ninety. And they're going to put her on our show?''

Nina chose to ignore Susan's continuing obsession with age; Robin chose to ignore Susan altogether.

''Not only May Minton, but Sylvia Kastle and Georgine Dyer as well,'' Nina said, quickly adding, ''They were also pretty big stars a while back, although not quite as big as May Minton.''

''And we're going to rename the show *Wrinkle City*,'' Robin said. ''What's going on here?''

''The same old story,'' Nina said. ''We're losing audience share points again. Or so they tell us. Frankly, I think it's just scare tactics, so we won't keep upping the ante when it comes to contract time. ''Anyway, somebody zeroed in on the popularity of *The Golden Girls* and decided we should do a rip-off. Only instead of Bea Arthur, Betty White, and Rue McClanahan, we'll have Minton, Kastle, and Dyer. As I understand it, a bit more than the cameos they'd planned at first. They'll be written in for just a few weeks, and then they'll be out. By then, or so the superbrains predict, the ratings will be up again and we'll see where we go from there.''

''It worries me,'' Robin said.

''Oh? Why?''

''All this sudden senior citizen chic. We've already got Angela Dolan and Mary Kennerly. Who needs any more tired blood than that?''

Nina laughed. ''Don't let Angela hear you. She'll

hang you by your thumbs. Mary Kennerly would shrug it off, but Angela . . .''

"Just how old do you think Angela is?" Susan interrupted. "I hear everything from forty to sixty."

"She could pass for forty on good days," Robin said, "but she usually manages to imply she's around forty-two. How far around, she doesn't say. But she really does take marvelous care of herself. I've heard that she once confessed she'd seen fifty, although I don't really believe she said it. And not even her worst enemy could accuse her of anything over fifty-five. Oh, who knows?"

On impulse, Nina said, "I'll just up and ask her, how's that? We're lunching today, la-de-da."

She was rewarded with stares from the other two. "How come?" Susan blurted.

"She asked me. That's how come. Now let's talk about something interesting."

Knowing she'd get no more out of Nina, Robin reverted to her lament. "Anyway, I think all this old-age stuff could work against us. After all, there are only so many jobs available in the soaps. And if they're being stolen by the prune people . . ."

"C'mon, Robin," Nina scoffed. "Since when don't our fans, male or female, love to look at pretty, young things like you? I think you're being silly. It's only an experiment. And it just might work. These great old girls could end up saving our necks."

"Since when have you been so high on grandmother types?"

"My mother may be a grandmother one of these days."

"Oh?" Robin raised an eyebrow. "Is this some sort of announcement? You and Dino getting serious?"

"Not at all." Nina went on instant guard, cutting short any casual speculations about her police detective boyfriend. "What I mean is that there's room for all of us. Besides, I'm crazy about May Minton. She's the nicest woman you'd ever want to meet."

"You *know* her?" Robin interjected.

"Yes, I know her. It's crazy, but *she* wrote *me* a fan letter once. Said I projected a marvelous authority." Nina mugged outrageously. "Such a wonderful judge of talent. Naturally, things just took off from there. We've met for lunch a few times. She's a real honey. So vital, so alert and with it."

"For her age," Susan added.

"Listen," Nina said. "The calendar isn't standing still for any of us. A little respect, if you please. Besides, I happen to know her true age, and you'd be surprised. They started a lot younger in those days."

"How do you know May Minton's age?" Robin demanded. "You're bluffing."

"I told you, we're friends. She let it slip one time when she got onto one of her nostalgia kicks. In fact, I'm visiting her tomorrow afternoon. She called to tell me she's getting butterflies; she wants a briefing on all the soap opera hocus-pocus I'm willing to share with her."

"Some people," Robin sniffed, "get all the breaks."

"Clean living," Nina said airily, "is what does it."

"That'll be the day," Susan retorted.

"Did somebody advocate clean living?" The question was preceded by a puff of smoke as Mary Kennerly joined the group. "Forget it. I tried it once. Doesn't work. Unless you want to be bored to death." They all shifted their chairs to make a place for the new arrival. As one of the oldest members of *The Turning Seasons*, Mary was also one of the most popular—not because of her age, but because under her gruffness on the surface, she was generosity itself with anything and everything, ranging from advice to the heartbroken to an endless supply of spare cigarettes.

"We were just talking about our upcoming guest stars," Robin said.

"Surely that wasn't sarcasm in your voice," Mary said, with a definite edge in hers. Nina decided to retire to the sidelines. "You think those ladies weren't stars? Don't kid yourself, and don't sell them short. They were bigger than I ever dreamed of being, and my dreams were so big I never even told my shrink about them. They could act the pants off you or me. And they *did* act the pants off any romantic lead they ever appeared with. Boy, the private files on those three . . ."

Nina watched with fascination as Robin and Susan struggled to frame delicately worded questions. But Mary adroitly passed the buck even before it got to her.

"Hey, Noel," she called across the room. "Come on over here and give the girls an eyewitness account of May Minton at her peak."

The senior actor of the cast crossed the room with a physical grace unusual in a man of his years. Ever since she first met Noel Winston, Nina had unconsciously considered him a sort of grandfatherly Cary Grant. But something different in his manner caught her attention at the moment. Usually delighted to be asked to share his storehouse of theater lore, Noel seemed instead to be the recipient of an unwelcome invitation, one that he accepted simply because he couldn't think of a reason to refuse.

"May Minton? Oh, there've been so many stories about her . . . who knows what's fact and what's fiction?"

That cut no ice with Mary Kennerly. "Come on, Noel. Give."

8

"What could I possibly tell you?" he said, defeated.

"You know—how she was to work with. And play with."

"Were you actually on stage with her?" Nina asked.

"Well—yes and no." They waited. They were prepared to wait all day if necessary. Noel heaved a long sigh and began. "You see, somewhere back in the Middle Ages she cast me in a minor role in *No Stranger Song*, which you've probably never heard of."

Robin and Susan were blank, but Nina and Mary smiled knowingly. The play Noel had mentioned was one of the longest-running Broadway hits of the forties. Nina often came upon references to it in her collection of theater books, and Mary had actually seen it with the original cast. That was what bothered her now.

"Hold it. I was there, Charlie, and I don't remember you being in that show."

"That's the point. I *wasn't* in it. It would have been the kind of early career break every young actor dreams about, but after two weeks of rehearsal I was replaced." Even now he looked pained at the memory.

"What happened, Noel?" Nina softly asked.

"It was a personal matter. It's not important now, after so many years." Nina thought his eyes were telling another story, one that still mattered very much. But he continued, as though to forestall further questions. "You asked what May Minton was like to work with. Well, she was a dream. Only in her mid-twenties, and an absolute goddess on stage. She was a wonder to work with because you learned so much from just being near her. But she was also

9

a terror because no member of the audience saw or heard any other actor while she was on stage."

"Were Sylvia Kastle and Georgine Dyer in the show, too?" Robin asked.

"No, no, those three didn't team up until later." Robin obviously had no knowledge of theater history. Noel decided to provide a crash course on the Minton years.

"May became a full-fledged theater name at the age of twenty-one," he said. Nina noted the familiar first-name reference, but let it pass. "Other smash hits followed—*The Mourning Dove, Appointment with Destiny, Days of Costanza,* and *The Trespassing Heart* were just a few. Then, in the fifties, she discovered a flair for musical comedy and set box-office records with shows like *Marry, Sweet Maids, Park Avenue Daze, Harry and Nell, Subway Serenade,* and *Gum-Drop Pie.* That one was the zaniest show I've ever seen." He seemed lost in a reverie. "Who'd have thought anyone so beautiful could be such an inspired clown? And still not lose one iota of her loveliness."

Noel fell silent for a moment, smiling at something unspoken, and then returned to his story. "So, a new Broadway season without May Minton was a dud indeed. Comedy or drama, she did it all. Her performance in *Passion and Power* won three National Theater Awards. You must have seen the film version."

"Oscar nomination, right?" Robin interjected.

"Right. She was robbed of that one. Anyway, she liked Hollywood and began to do more and more movies. Which led to television. She tried it with a few cameo roles, and soon she was doing leads on specials. Television somehow magnified her genius for comedy and she did a lot of broad slapstick, à la Lucille Ball. That was when she brought in Georgine Dyer and Sylvia Kastle. They'd each had respectable

10

careers of their own, but together the trio had the kind of chemistry that set audiences laughing before they even uttered a word. They did everything together—television, films, and then on to Broadway. They finally retired about fifteen years ago.''

Mary Kennerly looked at Noel oddly. ''You left out Tucker O'Brien,'' she said.

''He should be left out,'' Noel snapped.

''Nope. Too important.''

Nina curled up in her chair in a glow of contentment. This was what she loved best about the relaxed moments of her profession—when the older actors reminisced and told their stories of the great days, full of details and angles the theater books never provided. But along with the contentment she also felt a chill of apprehension; she remembered reading headlines about Tucker O'Brien even back in Madison, Wisconsin when she was still in her teens.

''Tucker O'Brien was one of Broadway's most brilliant directors,'' Noel continued, his tone taking on a darker color. ''He did a comedy with the three ladies, and then followed it with more serious plays. The result was that not only May Minton but Sylvia Kastle and Georgine Dyer as well became legends. *Farewell to October* could have run on Broadway forever; the movie grossed thirty-five million dollars. All three of them were financially fixed for life.''

He paused. Was that all? Nina wondered. ''Why did they retire?''

''Tucker O'Brien was found dead in his apartment one night in November, nineteen seventy-two. He'd been shot in the head. The murder was never solved, and there were some nasty rumors that one of the three women had killed him. Eventually they were completely cleared, of course.'' Abruptly, Noel stood up. ''What the devil is holding things up around here? Better go have a look." And he was gone.

Mary Kennerly stubbed out her cigarette thoughtfully. "There was a bit more to it than that," she said quietly. "Those rumors Noel mentioned were blown up by the press into full-fledged scandals. The columnists got their teeth into it and they had a field day. There was nothing that wasn't attributed to Minton, Kastle, and Dyer from murder and blackmail to backstage orgies. The public lapped it up—you know how they love to lick their chops over a fallen idol, and here were three to drool over. But nothing was ever proven and after a while people got bored by it and the press moved on to fresh targets. Even so, the ugly work was done, and though Minton, Kastle, and Dyer starred separately in various roles on stage, in movies, and on TV, they never appeared together again. Sylvia Kastle even had a nervous breakdown somewhere in that period. It was as if O'Brien's murder killed their friendship as well. By the mid-seventies, the threesome were no longer in demand. One by one, each of them announced her retirement.

"Dyer and Kastle went on to marry wealthy, influential men. Dyer's now the wife of Earnest Claypool, who's got a major say in city government. And Kastle is Mrs. Lance Kirby, meaning she owns large pieces of Manhattan real estate. You still see their names on the society pages once in a while. As for Minton, as far as I know she never married anyone. Really dropped out of sight."

Nina marvelled at the incredible coup Helen Meyer and her staff had engineered in coaxing Minton and Company out of retirement for a soap opera appearance, of all things. It would make show biz history. The TTS ratings were sure to zoom, and competing soaps would reel for months, fighting desperately to maintain viewer loyalty.

The luncheon with Angela Dolan was decidedly an event, especially for the overbearing Angela, who was making a concession of monumental proportions in extending the invitation in the first place. Even so, bowled over as she was, Nina McFall was still wary. Angela wanted something, and that was no mistake.

Today she was elegant in a crisp, lavender-gray silk suit with matching pumps, her silver-blond hair bound in a fetching scarf-turban of a deeper violet that ignited the blue in her eyes and made her hair sparkle in near-crystalline brilliance. Nina provided a startling contrast in her light woolen afternoon dress of creamy off-white worn with a pale green silk scarf and matching jewelry at the neck and wrists. Her flaming hair was gathered up on top of her head, with only a few tendrils escaping to frame her face—a stunning effect.

Eyes definitely popped when the chic duo had entered Claudine's, a classy French restaurant located on Seventieth.

Looking at Angela across the table, Nina found herself hoping she'd look as good at the same age— whatever it was. Rumor of a late-blooming romance in her life (with TTS producer Horst Krueger, of all people) had brought new bloom to her complexion, a new brightness to her cool, patrician gaze. Or was the revived vivacity only a result of the rumor, existing only in the beholder's eyes? It was a conjecture Nina fielded lightly, then let drop. Angela *was* looking great, dammit!

The waitress appeared and the two women ordered, Nina settling for the eternal chef's salad, An-

13

gela being more daring and indulging in a small cut of prime rib and a spinach salad.

As they awaited lunch, they sipped a light Chablis and made small talk, each guardedly appraising the other's outfit, makeup, and accessories. They were jockeying for psychological positions, marking time while each waited for the other to reveal something. Nina, especially, was eager for Angela to open up. And though she had a suspicion of what was bugging Angela, she mentally shrugged off her impatience. All in good time, she told herself.

The two TTS anchors were not actually enemies. Competitors would be a more appropriate way of describing their careful, touch-me-not relationship. Angela Dolan, trading on her twelve years with the show, did put on airs and gloried in her doyenne role at the TTS studio. And though Nina McFall had been a soaper for only five years and there were some in the cast with more seniority, it had quickly been accepted among the others, almost from the first, that the devastatingly beautiful redhead had star quality.

Accordingly, she had skipped a few grades and was now ranked on a par with Angela. The older woman was aware of this, and it bugged her mightily. She went out of her way to needle Nina at every possible opportunity, as a way of keeping this particular peasant in check.

It was a rivalry that Nina took lightly and rose to joyfully whenever the gauntlet was flung down. To her mind, a day without a jab from Angela was like a day without sunshine. The cast went silent at such times, watching expectantly when Nina's and Angela's paths crossed. The acid interchanges were a welcome shot in the arm to the routine-bored crew as well.

Small wonder that Nina had been astonished

14

when Angela had suggested lunch. It assumed the proportions of a milestone; all her colleagues were curious about the underlying reasons for the invitation and she knew they would pounce on her for details as soon as she got back. Nina, of course, would tell them something, but not everything. She had her games to play, too.

The verbal fencing continued. "Those colors do such wonderful things for your eyes," Angela said. Did Nina detect a note of sincerity? Was an olive branch being offered?

"Why, thank you, Angela. So nice of you to notice. That lavender suit is stunning. And the turban . . . *très élégante.* You certainly had heads turning as you entered."

Angela beamed. "Hardly. I'm sure they were looking at *you*, dear. But it's sweet of you to say so. And how have you been, Nina? After that dreadful thing in June, I mean. It must have been terrifying."

"Yes, it was," Nina replied. Through her mind raced a mercifully rapid fast-forward memory of the horrible deaths of *The Turning Seasons'* producer, Morty Meyer, and of his secretary, Gladys Parr. Morty had been poisoned and Gladys bludgeoned and thrown over a cliff. The frightening series of events in which Nina had participated and that led to the arrest of Byron Meyer, Morty's son by his first marriage, was something she didn't like to think about.

"I'm over it now, but it gave me nightmares for quite a while there. One thing I've learned, and that's to live for the day. You never know when you're going to make that final exit."

"How right you are, my dear." Angela paused. "But some good did come of it, I understand. How are you and your detective friend getting along?"

"No comment, Angela," Nina evaded. "I'm sure

15

you'll understand. Things are all very indefinite at this stage."

"I see." Angela smiled. "Well, I'll honor your reticence and wish you all the best. He'd be a fool to pass on someone as beautiful and charming as you."

Just then the waitress arrived with their order, and they chatted idly about their menu selections, all the while skirting the main issue. Until finally, with small talk exhausted and a stricken expression on her face, Angela came to the point.

"Nina, I'm sorry to trouble you with this, but I have no one else to turn to. We aren't close, I know, but maybe we should be. I'm not as formidable as I appear, nor am I as self-sufficient and secure as some people might think."

Nina was intrigued. "Angela, what is it? What's troubling you?"

Struggling to compose herself, Angela Dolan blurted, "Nina, I'm frightened. Things are happening, things beyond my ability to cope."

"Frightened? Why, Angela, whatever of?" And for the first time since she'd known the woman, Nina felt faint stirrings of real concern. It took guts for her ladyship to descend so abruptly from her high horse.

"This management brainstorm—the plan to bring in May Minton and her friends. It's really upsetting me."

"But why, Angela? It has to be one of the most brilliant moves Helen has ever made. It's a coup of the first order. We'll make show business history."

"Perhaps, Nina. But what will it do to *me*?" She broke off, attended her food. "There's . . . something you should know about me, Nina . . . I worry. I worry a lot. About my age, about the fact that my days as a star on *The Turning Seasons* are definitely numbered.''

''Angela, don't be foolish. You're a permanent star on the show, and don't ever think otherwise. Your role is secure.''

''I'll tell you something, Nina. Something I've never shared with anyone else. Promise me you'll honor this confidence. I'm older than most people think. I'm *not* forty-two. Or even forty-five. I've passed the half century mark, can you believe? But it's getting harder and harder to keep up appearances, to keep others from finding out. I'm getting tired of it.''

Nina quickly decided to take a soft, oblique approach to Angela's admission. Difficult though she was, she was worth more than the standard ''Surely you're joking! You can't be!'' response.

''I think you're overreacting, Angela. I'm sure you know that no one worth his salt ever lives without a feeling of insecurity ninety percent of the time. That's the wonderful thing about the soap opera world. Our fans become more loyal with every passing year. As we age, they associate with that, because they're getting older, too. No, Angela, your place on TTS is assured. You have absolutely nothing to be afraid of. Compared to May Minton and her friends, we're both ingenues; they aren't going to change a thing, other than our audience share. And that can only help all of us. So stop fretting, will you?''

''You're entitled to your interpretation of things, Nina,'' Angela countered, ''but I don't buy it. I view this as a threat. If Helen and Horst can arbitrarily juggle things around and try a radical departure like this, what crazy thing will they try next?

''The new wave might be an all-youth kick,'' Angela went on, ''or whatever solution they can come up with to prop up sagging ratings. This is only the beginning. And in the end they'll ticky-tacky the show to death. Even if May Minton's appearance does help our ratings, it's the beginning of the end. Helen will keep on experimenting and trying new things until she destroys us all!"

"Come now, Angela," Nina soothed, assessing the frantic look in the woman's eyes, "aren't you being a bit paranoid? I tell you, you're worrying needlessly. There will always be roles for mature women on the soaps, especially experienced actresses like you."

"Roles, yes. But *star* roles? The kind of roles I've become accustomed to? I don't want to end up being another Mary Kennerly, taking any 'white-hair' call they throw at me. I don't . . ." Angela broke off, stared into space.

Nina went silent as well. Despite the hard times Angela had given her, she knew the woman was sincerely worried, and not entirely without cause. Immediately, the old McFall knee-jerk compassion was at work, and she let herself inside Angela's head, empathizing with her in this moment of panic and self-doubt. Look, cupcake, she told herself, you'll be fifty-something yourself one of these days. If Angela has chosen to confide in you, has actually bared her soul, the poor thing's really terrified.

"Please, Angela," she coaxed, reaching across the table to take the woman's hand, "don't be so melodramatic. It's going to be okay. You'll see."

"It's easy for *you* to say," Angela replied, a hard edge forming on her voice. *"You're* young, you've got your whole life before you. But I . . ."

"You'll do just fine, Angela. Believe me. I know for a fact that even if this Minton shtick should catch on, it can't last. Neither May Minton nor the others is physically capable of doing it day in and day out, the way we do. And when she's forced to bow out, it can only strengthen your hand. You're the ones— you and Mary—who'll have to pick up the slack, fill the gap that'll be left."

Nina knew instantly she'd blundered! The implication that Angela and the decidedly older Mary Kennerly were in the same senior-citizen boat was a bad mistake. Instantly the fragile rapport that had built between them crumbled. Angela's eyes became flinty and Nina saw that she was questioning the wisdom of suggesting this luncheon in the first place, of letting her hair down and giving her younger colleague a glimpse of heretofore unseen vulnerability.

Abruptly the old Angela Dolan—belligerent, haughty and hard-nosed—was back. Nina could almost hear the steel gates crash down.

"I suppose, Nina," she said coldly, "that it's time we should be getting back. You *are* finished, aren't you?"

"Yes, I am," Nina said, forcing a smile. "You're right, it's that time."

Angela rose and sent an imperious glance around the elegant room. "Nina," she said coolly, "if you'd like to leave the tip . . ."

Nina stiffened. Of all the gall! she thought. Who invited who to this clambake? But she managed to retain her composure and dropped a ten dollar bill onto the table, making sure that Angela saw she was overtipping.

As they left the restaurant in silence, Angela carried her rage right along with her. She brushed off the hovering head waiter and ignored the doorman who quickly whistled up a cab for them. Nina quietly pressed the expected tips into their hands. I deserve it, she told herself. She trusted me with her pain and like a jerk I insulted her.

The ride back to the studio passed in silence. Nina watched ultra-expensive real estate flash past the window and gave herself over to some very dark thoughts about the pitiful state of the human condition.

Chapter Two

The next day, lolling in her tub and luxuriating in the prospect of a four-day weekend (thank God for being written out of the plot occasionally!), Nina looked forward to her afternoon appointment for drinks and giggles with May Minton. So May wanted Nina's advice on soap opera techniques! Fate could play weird and wonderful tricks.

Soaping a shapely ankle, Nina mentally reran one of her favorite scenes. Not one of the fantasies involving the devastating Dino—these were more and more becoming realities, anyway—but a scene that had actually happened: her first conversation with May Minton. Several months back, she'd been astonished to receive a personal note from the famous actress that was so flattering, it amounted to a fan letter. Even more amazingly, at the end were the words, "Let's get together for lunch or cocktails." And there, in her own hand, was May Minton's private phone number!

It took two days for Nina to gather up the courage to make the call. On the third try, she dialed all seven digits, still thinking, How can I? I can't. This is ridiculous. What will I say? This is nuts. What do you say to a legend? What if she . . .

"Yes? Who's calling?"

Nina's power of speech drained away at the sound of that voice. She'd heard it a hundred times in darkened movie houses and in the privacy of her own apartment when she ran a favorite tape on the VCR. It was as familiar and distinctive as Bankhead, Barrymore, Davis, or Hepburn. But coming directly into her ear that way, over the phone . . .

"Is anyone there, or is this one of those disgusting games? Come on now, phantom caller, either you speak up or I hang up."

Nina forced her voice to function. "Miss Minton? This is Nina McFall. You sent me a . . ."

A low, throaty laugh came through the phone. That laugh! And this time just for her! "Yes, I know what I sent you. How foolish you must think me. Well, put it down to a lifelong delight in recognizing real talent when I see it, which isn't too damn often these days."

"I . . . It was . . ."

"You don't know what to say. Of course not, real people often don't. Only phonies always know what to say. Or think they do. They gush like oil wells, and they're twice as slippery. But now I'm the one who's gushing, aren't I?"

"Not at all. It's . . ."

"Anyway, let's not waste time on the phone. I'd love to meet you. Come and have lunch with me. What day are you off?"

Nina was overwhelmed. "Lunch would be wonderful."

"Not if I cook it. We'll send out."

"I'm off for the next two days."

"Tomorrow, then. Do you drink?"

"Sometimes."

"Sometimes what?"

"Sometimes a little, sometimes a lot."

The famous voice cracked up in a whoop of laughter that made Nina feel like a blend of Neil Simon, Noel Coward, and Erma Bombeck.

"I'm going to borrow that. Helen will *love* it!" Helen who? Helen Meyer? Nina wondered. No, of course—Helen Hayes!

"Let's say one o'clock, then. My apartment, if you don't mind. We'll be able to talk without screaming. Unless we feel like screaming, in which case we'll damn well scream. Wasn't there a song about that?"

Nina scribbled down the address May Minton gave her, thinking that the actress made even a simple address sound like the most original line of dialogue ever written.

The next day as she approached Carson Place, the apartment building where May Minton lived, Nina was amazed to learn that the fluttery feeling known as stage fright could manifest itself outside the studio as well as inside.

But she needn't have worried. Once past the building's rigid security system, she ascended to the fifty-first floor in silent splendor and was greeted by an open door framing a full-length portrait of one of the theatre's immortals, regal in a floor-length gown of blue and gold brocade, with her long white hair swept up into a soft cloudy halo. Except that this was a living portrait.

No maid? No butler to usher her into the royal presence? May Minton was full of surprises, all of them pleasant.

"God almighty, the hair and skin are real! You're even more gorgeous in person. That cameraman of yours ought to be shot. Or if he's cute, send him over here—I'll think of some suitable punishment. Come on in, you must be starved. I cooked after all. Hope you like stuffed garbanzo beans. Only joking.

23

Can you uncork champagne? I always spray it all over the ceiling."

Nina started to giggle even before the door closed behind her, and the next three hours went by like a dream.

May's apartment was magnificent, containing a collection of stunning antiques and theatrical memorabilia. Champagne glass in hand, Nina was treated to a tour of the rooms with a running commentary on the origin of some of the items and most interesting mementos. Of particular interest to Nina was the wall of framed photographs in the living room—it included dozens of famous faces of the past, all either former co-stars or friends of May. Looking at them, Nina felt she'd stepped backward into a world of the theater as it used to be. Scattered around the room on every available surface were odds and ends that looked individually as though they belonged elsewhere, but which collectively seemed very much at home—a quill pen and crystal inkwell, a single lace glove, a long-handled wooden spoon, a fake pistol, an ornate brass telescope, a western belt buckle, a pair of pince-nez, and dozens more.

"Those are some of the props I used on the stage and in a couple of movies," May told Nina. "Looks like a junk shop, but they all mean something to me. Some retired actors keep watching their old movies over and over. Not this lady—I can't stand being reminded of how I used to look, and I only watch television for news and quiz programs. And your show, of course. Maybe I ought to get rid of all this garbage, but I'm too sentimental."

Each article had a story to go with it, and May was perfectly willing to tell them all. "Mostly they're just dust collectors, but I like to look at them. All except the telescope—I use that to check on the action in that building over there." Nina couldn't believe her ears. Was this one-time Great Lady of the Theater actually saying that she spied on people in their bedrooms? May saw the astonished expression on Nina's face and let out a whoop. "Listen, even an old lady needs a little boot once in a while. I'm not nosy, I'm jealous. Kind of like reliving old times. Anyway, no harm done and no one's the wiser. Come on, kid, drink up."

Nina had the impression May never stopped talking, but she knew that wasn't so because she remembered telling the vivacious old woman what amounted to the story of her life. It was amazing that she could find the nerve to relate such humdrum events to one of the world's most famous actresses—and even more amazing that the woman actually wanted to know!

"From what you've said, it sounds as though Madison, Wisconsin was the ideal place to grow up. How long did you teach school before the acting bug bit you?" May asked.

"Not long at all. Just a few years. Then somebody talked me into looking for theater work in Milwaukee."

"The big time!"

"So it seemed. I really loved it there, and the theater group I worked with was great . . . until one day I found myself flying to New York to try out for a part on the soaps. It was crazy! I didn't have any television background, my stage experience didn't really amount to much, I didn't have—"

"Stop right there. Forget about what you didn't have. It's what you *did* have that counted: brains, beauty, talent, luck, and a thick hide. And God help anybody who tries to get along in the theater without all five!"

"It was the luck that did it. I was so lucky, I never had to find out about the thick hide. I got the part."

"Certainly you did! You were the best one!"

"And I've been steadily employed ever since. For five years! Do you know how many actors work that steadily?"

"I think I have a pretty good idea."

Idiot! You've gotten so relaxed with this lady you've forgotten who she is and what she must have been through. You and your big mouth! Nina chided herself.

"That was dumb of me. Of course you know."

"Relax, and don't go all proper and polite on me. You have to say what's on your mind, or it doesn't work. I withdrew into this apartment years ago because I got so damned tired of people treating me like a sacred relic. I could see what was going on in their minds—careful what you say, she might get offended. Don't talk about this one or that one, they had a feud once. Or a love affair. Or, less likely, they *didn't* have a love affair." Nina started to giggle again. "Do you know that half the stories about me weren't true? Probably everyone knows that—they just don't know which half. Hang around, I might tell you."

By the time Nina left May Minton's apartment that first day, she had fallen in love with someone who wasn't only a great star of the past, but an incorrigible rip of today. And someone who, most likely, was very much in need of a friend. Despite her awestruck affection for May Minton, Nina was overwhelmed to realize she could be that friend.

And now, only a few months later, it seemed to be happening. She and May had gotten together for lunch or drinks roughly every two weeks since that first meeting, and their bond was growing steadily. To think that they might actually work together! Nina hoped Dave Gelber and Sally Burman would write some scenes between Melanie Prescott and

May Minton's character; as she dressed she wondered how she might engineer the writing of such
scenes, if necessary.

She chose an outfit of coordinated separates in
silk: a russet skirt falling just to the knee, a low-cut
blouse and softly shaped two-button jacket in russet
and cream stripes, accented by simple solid gold
button earrings and bangle bracelets. She gave herself a final check in the full-length bedroom mirror
and then, glancing out the window at the exciting
view of the Hudson from her thirty-sixth floor apartment, Nina was suddenly overcome with the facts
of her situation. Was she really, at thirty-four, a well-
known television actress earning $300,000 a year and
living in a deluxe Riverside Drive apartment? Most
incredible of all, was she really enjoying a delirious
love affair with the most gorgeous hunk of detective
on the New York City Police Department? Or was
she still only a schoolteacher from Wisconsin who
had escaped into a dream world? Or—was she a fig-
ment of her own imagination? Whatever she was,
she had to admit she liked it.

At the door, key in hand, she turned and swept
her gaze over the apartment. It was a shimmering
art-deco dream in peach, white, and chrome, fur-
nished and decorated with items of her own choos-
ing. No impersonal decorator had been at work here.
The Dunstan-Fowler armoire was there because she
liked it, not just because it was "right." The same
was true of the Buffoni davenport and, above it, the
Pearlstein painting (one of his typical leathery
nudes). It was a perfect apartment, viewed on a perfect afternoon.

Nina had been written out of Thursday's and Friday's shows, which meant she had only one script
to learn before her Monday morning call. A long,
glorious weekend loomed. Drinks that afternoon

with May, and then later she'd meet Dino and drive north to take in the glories of autumn in upstate New York. At Nina's insistence, Dino's twelve-year-old son by his first marriage would go along. They would shower Peter with attention, spoil him outrageously, and keep him on the move, so that on Saturday night, when Peter dropped into a deep, weary sleep . . . Dino, darling, the plans I have for you! What would it be like in the woods? In the rustic cabin they'd rented, all curled up together and cuddly in flannels . . . Oh, damn! Damn, damn, damn! She'd forgotten to buy a long flannel nightie. Her usual filmy nightwear number wouldn't do in a cabin in the woods, no matter how quickly she wriggled into it. And out of it . . .

She closed the door again and rushed to the phone. May answered on the second ring.

"May, it's Nina. This is so stupid, but I have to be a little late. I forgot to buy something I need for the weekend, and if I don't do it right now I'm going to forget again. Is three-fifteen all right?"

"Relax, honey, I'm not going anywhere and I won't start without you."

"I hate to keep you waiting."

"What are friends for? Get going, see you when you get here."

Nina took a cab to Bloomingdale's and naturally, because she was in a hurry, got stuck in traffic three times. For the same reason, she had to wait an extra ten minutes to pay for the luxuriously thick and soft, pink and white granny gown she selected. Finding another cab proved impossible, so she walked the five blocks to Carson Place on East Fifty-fourth Street, arriving slightly out of breath and totally out

28

of patience. It was 3:30, exactly an hour since she'd phoned May.

At the entry to the elaborate and overdone lobby of May's building, the uniformed doorman swung open the massive steel and glass door, sending an admiring glance at Nina's outfit, paying particular attention to her long, sleek legs. Another guard, stationed at a command post desk equipped with various electronic surveillance devices, asked the invariable question: Who did she wish to see?

"May Minton," Nina responded with a blinding smile, feeling very good about herself this day. "She's in apartment fifty-one-twenty."

The guard, a tall, gaunt specimen, double checked the apartment number by punching it into the computer keyboard before him. "That's correct, ma'am," he announced as the information instantly popped onto the screen. He picked up his phone. "Who shall I say is calling?"

"Nina McFall." She wondered if the name would register with the man.

Apparently he didn't watch soaps; there wasn't the slightest blink of recognition. "I'll ring her," he said.

After eight rings, he turned back to Nina. "She doesn't seem to be answering, Ms. McFall."

"That's funny," Nina said, frowning. "I spoke to her on the phone just a little while ago. She's expecting me. Perhaps she's occupied. Try again, will you?"

The security man rang May Minton's number several more times, with the same result. "I'm sorry, Miss. She must have gone out."

"Have you been on duty all afternoon?" Nina asked. "Did you see her go out?"

"I've been here since eight this morning. If she went out, I'd certainly have noticed."

Nina became alarmed. "Please keep ringing. She's got to be there." She was picturing the elderly actress lying on the floor of her apartment, victim of a fall, or even worse, a heart attack. "Oh dear, if anything's happened to her . . ."

Three more minutes of repeated ringings brought no response. By then the security guard was equally concerned.

"We've got to get up there—fast," Nina said, switching into her take-charge mode. She suddenly thought of May's fondness for champagne. Maybe she *had* started without her, drank too much and passed out. "If she's fallen or something . . . We don't have any time to waste. You do have a pass key, don't you?"

"No, ma'am, I don't. We're not authorized to go onto any of the floors. I'd lose my job if I left my desk." Then, moving decisively, he tapped in another number. "I'll call Mr. Maxey, the resident manager. He'll take charge."

Two minutes later Maxey, a portly, balding man of roughly forty-five, emerged from the elevator. "Ms. McFall?" he said, a bit officiously, as if impatient at being drawn away from vastly more important chores. "I'm Ronald Maxey. How may I help you?"

"I had an appointment with Miss Minton in fifty-one-twenty. She was expecting me at about three-fifteen. It's now three-thirty-five. I spoke to her only an hour ago and she was all right then. Can you get into her apartment?"

He didn't answer, but instead stared hard at Nina. "Ms. McFall?" he said. "I have a feeling I know you from somewhere. Have we met?"

"If you watch soap operas, you might know me. I'm on *The Turning Seasons*."

His smile became obsequious. "Yes, of course. I

have seen you on the show. When things get slow in the office, I sometimes indulge. What a pleasure, Ms. McFall!''

''Please, Mr. Maxey, can we get on with this? I'm sure something's happened to May. Older women can be accident-prone, you know.''

''Yes, of course, Ms. McFall. If you don't mind, it's best that I go up alone. If there's been an accident, I'll inform you.''

Nina's eyes flashed. ''But I *do* mind,'' she announced, slipping into her Melanie Prescott characterization. ''I'm going up there with you. She's my friend, after all.'' She fixed him with a baleful glare. ''And it definitely would be more discreet, Mr. Maxey, if a *woman* were along. You do know what I mean.''

Maxey flushed. ''Yes, of course, Ms. McFall. That *would* be wise. If you'll follow me.'' He looked back at the security guard. ''Keep off that phone as much as you can, Sam. Get Dr. Bradley's phone number up on the computer, just in case.''

Together he and Nina hurried toward the elevator.

Arriving on the fifty-first floor, they stood before the ornately framed, reinforced steel door of apartment 5120. Anxiously Maxey pushed the buzzer, then took a few tentative whacks at the door with the flat of his hand, but there was no response.

''Please,'' Nina urged as he continued pushing the button, ''use your key. It's obvious that something's wrong.''

Obviously resenting Nina's take-charge manner, Maxey reluctantly reached inside his suit jacket and brought out a small plastic card, which he inserted into the specially designed computerized lock. The overriding numbers hummed through the intricate electronic coding and there was a solid *thunk-thunk* as the bolts fell aside.

A moment later Maxey turned the knob and slowly pushed the door open.

They both stood motionless for a few seconds, their eyes sweeping first the small foyer, then the spacious, sunlit living room beyond. Insofar as either of them could detect, the apartment was deserted. Could it be? Nina speculated, a sinking feeling in her stomach. Had May Minton gone out on a sudden errand? But if so, how had the guard missed her departure?

Nina was the first to move into the apartment, treading softly, almost afraid that May might appear at any moment to challenge this invasion of her private sanctum.

Standing dead center in the huge room, studying the doors leading to different living areas, she was surprised at the oddly pristine order, as if the aging star's quarters were awaiting inspection. May's apartment usually looked more lived in, not ready to be photographed. Certainly there were no signs of a break-in, or of an accident of any sort.

"Everything looks fine to me," Maxey stated.

"Shhh," Nina cautioned, turning her head. "I thought I heard something. Back in there."

They both moved cautiously into the corridor leading to the two bedrooms and bathrooms. Again Nina heard the sound and waved Maxey to a halt. Then she identified the sound.

"False alarm," she sighed gratefully. "May's taking a shower. That's why she couldn't hear the phone."

"Thank God for that," Maxey grumbled. "All I need is an accident on the premises."

But even as the words came out, Nina had second

thoughts. No, something wasn't right. It wasn't like May to forget their appointment and take a shower instead.

A sudden cold chill swept her body, covering her arms and back with goose bumps.

Immediately Nina rushed down the hall, opened the door to May's bedroom, then paused before the door of the master bath. The thrumming of the shower was louder now. "May!" she called, banging the door with her fist at the same time. "May, it's Nina! Are you all right?"

Again she fell silent to listen. She heard only the sound of furiously rushing water.

Maxey, standing discreetly in the bedroom doorway, smiled weakly and shrugged. It's your show, his expression said. There's no way I'm going into that bathroom.

Nina pounded again. "May!" she cried, more loudly, more desperately now. "Can you hear me? It's Nina!"

Dear God, she wailed inwardly. She must have fallen in the shower. Knowing that too much time had already been wasted, she decisively turned the knob and pushed the door open.

A blinding cloud of steam rushed from the bath and expanded out into the bedroom. Nina paused briefly to give the steam time to begin to dissolve, then plunged forward.

"May?" she called one last time. Then, steeling herself, she reached up and slowly drew the heavy, tulip-patterned shower curtain aside.

What she saw froze her blood.

There, at the bottom of the tub, almost completely submerged, lay May's body, naked, with long trails of white hair plugging the drain, forming a crude stopper. The hands floated limply at the body's side.

Final curtain. The words flashed into Nina's brain. But, God, no! Nobody should go out like this.

"Don't come in here!" she said over her shoulder to Maxey. "May wouldn't want anyone seeing her like this."

Moving like a robot, she leaned over and turned off the shower faucets. The sudden silence was deafening. She forced aside a wave of queasiness and reached into the hot water to gather May Minton's hair and pull it away from the drain. Instantly the water began gurgling down the pipes.

Blessedly, the dead woman's eyes were closed. But the mouth was open in a fishlike gape, frozen in an eternal expression of surprise. Fleeting thoughts of first aid, of CPR crossed Nina's mind. But when she realized how heavy the body was, saw the way the head lolled so helplessly, she promptly rejected any emergency measures. May Minton was dead, and nothing anyone could do would bring her back.

As a gesture of decency and respect, Nina held May's shoulders up until the water had completely drained from the tub. Then she gently lowered her back to the porcelain. There was no way in the world that she could have lifted the waterlogged body from the tub by herself.

Her breath coming in shallow gasps, Nina stood over the tub, studying the pallid flesh. Is this how it always happens? she questioned dully. Must death be so ugly? This famous, brilliant woman, a woman who had made millions laugh and cry surely deserved a more dignified end.

May, she whispered inwardly. Dear May . . .

The poor woman, she commiserated. She must have gone into the shower just after I called. Perhaps the stress caused by thoughts of her upcoming TV comeback had been too much for her heart. Or

34

maybe she'd simply slipped and fallen, hitting her head on the faucet as she'd gone down, unable to save herself.

But there had been no trace of blood in the water, had there? Nina didn't recall seeing any. Perhaps she shouldn't have let the water flow out. Too late now. Dear Lord, what would Dino say?

But even through her sense of shock, Nina had an insistent feeling of inconclusiveness. No, she told herself, it's too pat; that's exactly what someone wants me—the world—to believe. That May Minton fell in the tub and knocked herself out. That she had drowned accidentally.

And if that line of reasoning were to prevail, then someone would very possibly be getting away with homicide.

Nina, stop! she commanded herself sharply, trying to overcome the paranoid conjecture. You've got murder on the brain!

She spun around and left the bathroom. She was almost surprised to see the manager still standing there, a puzzled expression on his face.

When he saw the sick look on Nina's face he said, "Ms. McFall? What is it? What's hap—"

"Don't touch anything," she ordered in a quavering voice, her eyes haunted. "And don't move around any more than you absolutely have to."

The man watched with wondering eyes as Nina picked up an ornate French telephone and carefully dialed.

Then the worst of Ronald Maxey's fears came true, as he heard the tense young woman ask for Detective Dino Rossi.

"Dino? It's me, Nina." She paused, fought for control. "I hate to tell you this, but it's happened again. Dino, I think there's been another murder."

35

Chapter Three

Detective-Lieutenant Dino Rossi commanded a special squad that had been set up for the express purpose of dealing with what the gentlemen at One Police Plaza quaintly termed "celebrity crimes." Another monicker pinned on the unit was the "Silk-Stocking Squad."

Though the Inspector General had initially considered the unit someone's idea of a practical joke, its case load from the very outset had always been full.

Broadway types, television personalities, musicians, and opera singers were prime targets for crime. If they weren't being bashed, murdered, or ripped off by opportunistic scuzz-artists, they were conning one another.

Thus it had been appropriate for Nina McFall to contact Dino Rossi upon finding May Minton dead in her Carson Place apartment. Add to this their working relationship in the Morty Meyer slaying several months earlier, and the protocol was correct indeed. And considering their remarkably close personal relationship, it wasn't surprising that Rossi, flanked by Sergeant Charley Harper and three members of the crime-scene unit, showed up only twenty minutes after Nina called. The sirens and flashing lights atop the radio cars parked at the main entrance to Carson Place did little to enhance the prestigious tone of that exclusive establishment.

"I suppose I shouldn't have moved her, drained the tub or anything, Lieutenant," Nina apologized as she escorted Rossi and Harper into the bathroom, "but it was such a shock. I thought she might still be alive, that I might be able to help her."

"It's all right, Ms. McFall," he reassured her, both of them falling back on a previously-agreed-upon formality in public situations. "Fingerprints are tough to find when a shower's been running full-force for an hour. You did just fine."

Hardened though he was to violent death, it invariably gave Rossi a wrench when a woman was involved. Both he and Harper fought to control their expressions, to keep revulsion in check. They studied the scene for long minutes, until, finally satisfied, Rossi wordlessly draped a towel over May Minton's pathetic form.

Briefly the two investigators poked about in the bathroom proper, surveyed the dead woman's toiletries, all in meticulous order. They examined the bathrobe that was draped over a small, brass-finished wire chair. Nina looked at May Minton's bedroom slippers, standing in precise formation under the chair. She again had the fleeting thought that everything in the apartment was just too neat. It was as if someone had arranged everything meticulously, as if they wanted to create an impression of orderly preparation for the shower. Dressing the stage was something she knew about.

It was the same in May's bedroom. There, neatly arranged on the bedspread lay a navy-blue caftan, lingerie, and hose, all awaiting her return from the shower. A pair of black pumps stood at attention on the floor beside the bed. All her bureau drawers were closed, the closet doors shut. Maybe I'm paranoid, Nina mused, but something's definitely fishy. May just wasn't a fussy kind of person. But she kept silent. This was Dino's professional turf; let the observations come from him.

But they didn't come. After a cursory scan of the room, Dino Rossi turned back. "Okay," he called over his shoulder to the men from the crime-scene unit who waited in the living room. "Jake and Paul, get in here. Get going on that bathroom." Gently he edged the white-faced Nina from May's bedroom. "We can talk out in the other room, Ms. McFall."

In the spacious living room Dino and Nina sat on the largest of the three couches. On another, Harper interrogated Ronald Maxey. Meanwhile, another member of Rossi's team dusted the kitchen and hallway for fingerprints and sought any possible signs of violence.

Patiently, never raising his voice, Rossi led Nina back to square one. How had she come to know May Minton? What had brought her to the woman's apartment this particular afternoon?

As Nina answered the questions, she kept up the pretense of a formal business relationship with Rossi, but she allowed part of her attention to focus on the fact that she was deliriously in love with this tall, dark, moody, broad-shouldered, and fiercely independent detective. She wondered how she'd ever gotten along without him. And at the moment, she'd have liked nothing better than to turn the clock back a few hours, cancel her appointment with May Minton, and drag him off to her bedroom. Goddamn it all! Was this nightmare going to ruin their weekend in the woods? Instantly, she felt contrite for harboring such trivial thoughts. She'd lose a romantic weekend—so what? Poor May had lost her life. Nina shifted her focus completely to the business at hand.

"On the phone, you reported this as a possible murder," Dino was saying. "How did you arrive at that conclusion? Going by first impressions, I'd say it was an accidental death." She studied the set line of his jaw and knew how much he wanted this to be an accident.

"I know you're going to laugh, but I just have one of my hunches. Something simply doesn't add up."

"Elaborate, please."

"I just don't feel right about it," she said, ignoring his indulgent smile. "I called May at about two-thirty to tell her I'd be a little late. She seemed perfectly calm, exactly as usual. In fact, she said that whenever I arrived, she'd be ready." Her look was rueful. "Only, of course, I wasn't ready. The story of my life."

"Go on."

"Well, does it sound right to you? If she was ready when I called, why would she change her mind a half hour or so later and decide to take a shower?"

"Yeah, you're right," Rossi said absently, his brow furrowing. "Something doesn't jibe there. When you got here, did the security guard say anything about Miss Minton having any visitors between the time you called and the time you arrived? An hour had passed by then. Plenty of time for someone to come and go."

"No, he didn't. But then, if someone had been to see May, there's no reason he would have mentioned it to me."

Rossi looked up. "Charley," he barked to his assistant, "get that security man up here. Right now."

"Another thing," Nina offered, sounding as casual as possible. ''Didn't that scene in the bathroom as well as the bedroom look like a setup to you?''

Rossi frowned. ''What are you talking about?''

''May's clothes, her shoes, the bedroom slippers. Everything so very, very neat, as if she was getting ready for an inspection or something. Doesn't that puzzle you?''

''Maybe she was a neat woman.''

''But she wasn't—or at least, not *that* neat. It simply is out of character for everything to be so precisely arranged.''

Rossi looked skeptical. ''So she decided to straighten up a little while she waited for you,'' he said, dismissing her observations. ''Let's get on with this.''

Nina felt piqued, but held her temper in check. Perhaps Dino was right and she was going off the deep end on this point.

''You know how this goes, Nina. Step by step. Tell me every single detail you can think of from the time you arrived until now. Your gut-level impressions—how the security man acted, how Maxey acted. You never can tell what might turn up.''

Nina got as far as the moment when she had hesitated outside May Minton's bathroom, when the cadaverous-looking guard arrived.

Dino jotted the man's name, address and phone number in his notebook. ''Tell me, Mr. Nastasi,'' he began, ''did Miss Minton have any other visitors today? Especially just before Ms. McFall got here?''

Nastasi considered carefully. ''I don't think so. But to be absolutely positive, I'd have to pull it up on the computer. We're required to enter the name of every visitor we admit.''

''But to the best of your recollection, she'd had no other visitors today?''

''None.''

"Do you recall seeing her go out? Might she have returned with someone, taken that party upstairs with her?"

"Nope. Miss Minton was a very solitary person. She seldom went out, seldom had guests. I'd remember a thing like that."

"Good so far," Rossi said. "Now how about other visitors this afternoon? To other apartments? Say, within the last hour or two?"

"Again, I'd have to check the computer. But offhand I remember only two or three—it's been kind of a slow afternoon. Two men and a woman. There was a short guy with a mustache who came in perhaps three quarters of an hour before Ms. McFall, but he went up to the Gregg Dalmani apartment on the forty-second floor."

"Speaking hypothetically, is it possible that this man might not have gone to the place he said, but to Miss Minton's door instead and somehow gained admittance?" Rossi asked.

Nastasi mulled that one over for a moment. "Well, I called Mr. Dalmani. He said to send the gentleman up; he was expecting him."

Rossi turned to the rental manager. "Am I correct in assuming, Mr. Maxey, that once a person passes Mr. Nastasi's station and gets into the elevator, he can get off on any floor he chooses and visit whomever he likes?"

Maxey shrugged. "Yes, I suppose that's possible. We can't follow every visitor wherever he goes. Once they're admitted to the elevator, they're pretty much on their own."

"And what about those TV monitors I saw on my way in? How do they work?"

"They're on a timer," Maxey explained. "They give the security guard a ten-second glimpse of each of the thirty residential levels. There are five monitors that give us a looksee down each hallway every few minutes.''

"So it's possible that someone could enter under false pretenses as long as someone cleared him, and wander around—and your cameras might miss that person?''

"Yes,'' Maxey said, squirming. "I guess that's possible. We'd need thirty cameras to avoid that. And how could one man monitor thirty screens? Our people have a hard-enough time with five.''

Rossi addressed the security guard. "Did you, Mr. Nastasi, see anyone wandering around on the fifty-first floor? Outside Miss Minton's door, perhaps?''

"No,'' the man said, averting his gaze. "I didn't. But like Mr. Maxey says, it could have happened when the cameras were panning the other floors.''

Rossi's voice carried a hint of accusation. "Could it be possible, Mr. Nastasi, that you admitted some unauthorized visitor into the elevator?''

Nastasi stiffened, his face flushing angrily. "No, sir!'' he said. "We've got our rules. Nobody goes up without the tenant's permission.''

"Lieutenant,'' Maxey snapped, "I resent this line of questioning. All our employees are bonded, double-checked and perfectly trustworthy. As Sam said, he'd lose his job in ten seconds if he tried something like that.''

Rossi smiled and gave Maxey a dismissive wave. "Just routine, Mr. Maxey. We have to ask.'' He turned to the guard. "Thanks, Mr. Nastasi. I think that'll do it for now. Please make a list of all today's visitors for us, including the times they entered and left. You can go now.''

He gestured to Harper to continue his interview with Maxey. "Now, Ms. McFall,'' he said with crisp authority, "if we can take up where we left off?''

42

Nina smiled at Dino and moved to the far end of the room. He looked so terrific today, there was such a strong aura of authority about him. Could this be the same man who kissed her so gently, whose caresses sent her to the stars? Once again she directed her thoughts to more appropriate channels. She was particularly impressed with the way Dino had handled the security guard, hitting him with that last question when he was least expecting it. Had the man acted suspicious at that moment, or was her imagination working overtime?

"What about it, Nina?" he said, joining her at the windows where Harper and Maxey couldn't possibly hear them. "There has to be something behind all this. Tell me some more about the plan to put her on your show. How were the other actors at the studio taking all this?" he asked.

"Not too well. Soapers—we're all paranoid." She laughed. "As you well know, we tend to see demons behind every flat."

"And how do *you* feel about writing those old-timers into the script?"

"It's a brilliant move. It'll give the show a badly needed shot in the arm. And it would have been wonderful to have worked with May and her friends on a daily basis. The things I could have learned . . ." Nina sighed.

"You're certainly a charitable type."

Nina flashed him a brief smile. "Oh, yes," she said, "I certainly am. I help old ladies across the street, feed stray dogs . . ."

"Anybody in particular making waves?" Dino asked now.

"Oh, the younger cast members . . . even Robin . . . are afraid that the emphasis on age will freeze them out, and the older ones are afraid someone will steal their thunder."

"For instance? As if I didn't know."

"Angela Dolan, of course. She even took me to lunch and laid a tale of woe on me."

Dino laughed. "She finally let the moths out of her billfold?"

"Yes, miracles do happen. But she reverted to type at the end."

"And?"

"She stuck me with the tip. Confucius say, 'There is no free lunch,' and Confucius damn right."

"You screwball!" He grinned at her, then asked, "What was Angela's main groan?"

"She's getting too old for these constant disruptions on the set. She was afraid of losing her job, afraid May would cause her to be written out of the show. Oh, she really carried on."

"As bad as that, huh?"

"As bad as that. She even broke down and nearly admitted her real age. Now *that's* serious."

"And how old *is* she?"

Nina feigned hauteur. "No comment, Lieutenant."

"Well, pardon me all to Hell."

"Of course. All the way and back again."

Just then Sergeant Paul Wiley, one of Dino's special team, beckoned Rossi into the bedroom. Nina watched the door close behind him and cast her eyes around the room.

She moved over to the wall of framed photographs that always fascinated her. She marvelled at the familiar faces looking back at her, frozen forever at the height of their youth, their talent, their fame. Nina was able to identify almost all of them, and the few whose names she couldn't remember she recognized anyway. She'd have to look them up in her collection of "Theater World" annuals when she got home. What a life! And what a tragedy.

The mood of nostalgia snapped the moment Dino returned from his conference with Wiley. His expression was as dark as she'd ever seen it.

"Looks like murder one," he announced grimly. "The guys found the back of her skull caved in. More of a dent than a simple fall would cause. Unless the medical examiner finds water in her lungs, which at this point I doubt, my guess is that May Minton was bludgeoned to death. You called it again, honey."

A cold tremor swept over Nina. "I can't say that I'm exactly filled with pride." Her voice broke. "God, what am I—some kind of lightning rod for murder and mayhem?"

Rossi's voice was deep and comforting. "This kind of crap happens. Don't go blaming yourself." He sighed. "Hide-and-seek time again."

Nina fought back tears. "Oh, Dino, who'd murder such a wonderful woman? What did she ever do to deserve it?"

"My thoughts exactly. Okay, Miss Marple. I figure it's probably connected with this role on TTS. She's been out of the limelight fifteen years and nobody's bothered her. But the minute she comes out of retirement—no more May Minton."

"It does seem like more than mere coincidence."

"Somebody on the show could have been scared enough to make sure that May Minton never got line one out of her mouth. Any candidates?"

Nina thought. "Yes, it sounds like May's comeback could have something to do with it. But we mustn't go off half-cocked. I'm sure there are possibilities we haven't even thought about yet. May's murder may be entirely unrelated to anything or anyone at *The Turning Seasons*."

"Angela Dolan," Dino persisted, "has a perfect motive for wanting May Minton gone. The guard

said a woman was admitted shortly before you arrived; you heard him."

"Two men were also let in," Nina replied. "But
until we identify them, find out what they were doing here, who they were seeing, if they were even
remotely connected with May . . . Let's not leap to
improbable conclusions."

The minor put-down dented Rossi's ego, just
enough to put an edge into his voice. "Improbable
or not, it's the most logical lead we have. Like I said,
until this TTS role came along, Minton hadn't had
so much as a case of the sniffles. I just hope that
Angela's got a good alibi."

"Call her," Nina said, letting the exasperation
show. "I'm sure you'll find she was at the studio,
taping all afternoon."

"So she's got an accomplice doing her dirty work
for her. It's been done before—if you'll think back."

Suddenly Nina had a sick, cold feeling in her
stomach. "Please, Dino. Let's not argue. I'm sorry,
but I don't agree with you. And you're too good a
detective to go jumping to conclusions like this."

"So?" he challenged, his voice still edgy. "Who
do *you* think did it? That's all I'm asking."

"Oh, Lord, darling," she said, "it could be a
dozen people. What do we know about May Minton, really? Yes, she came across as a wonderful,
feisty old lady. But she's been in show biz all her
life, and that's no bed of roses. How many unsavory
people do you imagine might be lurking in the background of her life? Would there be someone in those
archives who'd like to see her dead? Any old lovers?
Or jealous, vengeful women whose lovers she might
have stolen way back when?

"That scandal in nineteen seventy-two, when
Tucker O'Brien, that director, was murdered—there

46

might still be some flak from that flying around. Some skeletons just won't stay buried.''

"Oh? Tucker O'Brien? What's that all about?''

Nina related what she knew about the O'Brien murder.

"Yeah,'' Rossi said, rubbing his chin reflectively, "that's an angle, all right. It looks like we've got our hands full.''

"What do you want me to do?'' Nina asked.

"Honor our partnership agreement by continuing to be my eyes and ears at the studio,'' Rossi said promptly.

"Think that'll be any help? Seems to me I blew my cover there during our last caper.''

"All you can do is try. Anything that doesn't look kosher to you, just give a shout.'' His eyes grew grave. "But promise me. No Nancy Drew stuff. No sticking your neck out, understand?''

Nina forced a grin. "I suppose. But, as I recall, some of those things I didn't initiate; they came looking for me.''

"You know what I mean. Just keep your nose clean and keep me posted on whatever happens at the studio.''

"Yes, Daddy.''

"Don't be cute.''

"And just what do you suppose is going to happen at the studio that might be worth reporting?''

"Something to do with Angela, I'll bet.''

"Will you stop? I'm starting to regret I ever mentioned her. Yes, she was running scared, but not *that* scared. Besides, she doesn't have the smarts, let alone the muscle to arrange to have someone murdered. She can be infuriatingly dense, but I still like her for some crazy reason. Believe me, the sooner you drop that angle, the better off you'll be.''

"Okay, I'm dropping it—for now. You convinced

me. But tell me this, what's going to happen at Meyer Productions now, with May Minton dead?''

''That's hard to say, Dino. When I think of all the script pages that have been written, how they've revamped the whole story line for weeks to come . . . I don't see how they can just ditch the project.''

''What options do they have?''

''I suppose they could go along with the concept—bring in Sylvia Kastle and Georgine Dyer just the same. Maybe they can find some other old star to play May's role. That sounds logical.''

''Won't the bad publicity kill them?''

''In this business, no publicity is all bad. Once it hits the papers, people might tune in just to see the woman who takes the role May Minton was supposed to play. And once we get them hooked—'' She smiled wanly, nodded her head. ''Yes, I think that's the way it'll play. That's what I'd do if I were in Helen Meyer's shoes. In fact, I'd run with it.''

Nina flashed a cagey grin. ''Hey,'' she said in a faraway voice, ''you don't suppose Helen murdered May to get all that free ink? I wouldn't put it past her! Thinking . . .'' she tapped her head, ''always thinking . . .''

Rossi recognized the put-on. ''All right, Nina. Have your fun. And while you play games . . .''

He rose from the couch and went to where Harper was still questioning Ronald Maxey. ''Bad news,'' he told the manager. ''We can't be certain until we have the medical examiner's report, but it may well be that Miss Minton was murdered. It's probable that she was put into the tub to make it look like she drowned after a fall.''

Maxey went pale. ''My God!'' he said. ''Poor Miss Minton! She was one of our best tenants. Never bothered anybody. Everybody loved her.'' Then more disturbing thoughts entered. ''Oh, Jesus, the publicity! There'll be police and reporters all over the place. I'll never be able to rent this apartment once the word gets out. Tell me, Lieutenant, will all this have to be released to the press?''

But Rossi wasn't listening. Now he approached team member Kyle Jagedorn, who was on his hands and knees, peering beneath a huge bookcase. ''Hey, Jag,'' he said, ''looks like we got a basher here. Probably murder one. See if you can come up with anything that might have served as a weapon. A heavy ashtray, a lamp, anything.''

Jagedorn, a slight, blond-haired man of thirty-five, looked up at his boss, his eyes grim. ''Ain't that a bitch,'' he said. ''A nice old broad like May Minton. I saw her on a TV rerun the other night. Almost had me bawling. Who ya' gonna trust when they start clubbing people like her?''

He struggled to his feet. ''I'd better go down and get the vacuum. We'll be needing hair and dust samples before we're through, that's for sure.''

As Jagedorn started out the door, the medical examiner's crew arrived with a body bag and stretcher. Nina grimly watched the two men go into the bathroom; she heard faint gruntings and thumpings. Minutes later, they bore the stretcher out, May Minton's body encapsulated in the dark gray plastic shroud.

Why May? Of all people, why did it have to be May Minton?

Dumb luck, came the reply. And much as she hated the flippancy, Nina recognized that sarcasm was her best defense at the moment, or she just might dissolve in tears.

It was clear that Kyle Jagedorn and his vacuum would be gathering microscopic bits of possible evidence for some time, so Dino suggested that Maxey see Nina down to the lobby. With Maxey hovering nearby, they parted formally; neither of them mentioned their weekend plans.

Nina climbed into a cab and gave the Primrose Towers address. It seemed like only moments later that she found herself sitting in front of her television set, watching but not hearing the late news. Hours had gone by, during which she'd automatically ridden home, paid the cab driver, gone up to her apartment, changed, prepared and eaten dinner, and settled down for an evening of video.

But she didn't recall a second of it except for the livid emphasis with which the announcers handled the news of the Minton murder. Throughout, she'd been mentally rerunning the entire afternoon, from the moment she entered the lobby of Carson Place to the second she left it.

Something was bothering her. Something was wrong. Something was *missing*. But what? Well, the best way to pry a buried thought out of your mind is to concentrate on something else. So she took a few old copies of "Theater World" from her bookshelves and amused herself by identifying the few people in May Minton's photo gallery whose names had escaped her. But she found it very hard to keep her eyes open. . . .

Nina awoke from a sound sleep, turned off the blank television screen, and picked up the book that had slid to the floor. Bingo! Abruptly wide awake, she resisted the urge to phone Dino. She had a question to ask him, but decided it could wait until morning. Besides, she was certain he couldn't possibly know the answer.

Chapter Four

If Nina McFall had entertained thoughts of being left to her own devices on Friday, such were summarily blasted when her phone rang at 8:30 A.M. In her kitchen, still in her morning daze, groping her way toward something vaguely resembling breakfast, the sound was especially jarring. Myrna Rowan, the main administrative slavey of TTS, was on the line.

"Hate to do this to you, Nina," she said brightly, "on your day off and all. Orders from headquarters—Mr. Krueger's called an emergency meeting at eleven o'clock sharp. You *will* be there." She laughed nervously. "I expect that it has to do with the May Minton murder. Wasn't that a shocker? For you, especially. You certainly didn't need that."

"No," Nina agreed, "I certainly didn't." How, she asked herself, had her involvement in the case gotten into the pipeline so quickly?

"I don't suppose I can get out of it?"

"You could send a death certificate," Myrna suggested.

"Okay, I'll be there. Under protest, but I'll be there."

As soon as she finished the call with Myrna, Nina called Dino.

"Hi. Did I wake you? How did you sleep? I have a question."

"Good morning yourself; no, you didn't; fine; what's the question; and who is this?"

"Very funny! Remember yesterday, when Wiley called you into the bedroom?"

"Vividly. I always get excited when someone calls me into a bedroom."

"My, aren't we full of beans this morning. Dino, I'm in a hurry. Horst has called a special meeting, probably connected with May's death, and I have to be at the studio by eleven. Now do you want to listen to this or not?"

"I'd listen to you anytime, anyplace. What kind of sweet somethings do you have for me this morning?"

"While you were in there, I sort of browsed around the living room, and I went through that photo gallery on the wall near the windows."

"What did you find?" The bantering tone was gone.

"It's what I *didn't* find. It nagged at me for hours, and then it hit me. Those photographs cover her whole career. There are pictures of May with every major star she ever worked with. Except one. Want to guess?"

"No. Just tell me."

"Sylvia Kastle."

There was a brief silence from Dino's end of the line.

"I guess that's a little odd," he said, without much conviction.

"A *little* odd! Dino, May Minton had some of the biggest hits of her career with Sylvia Kastle and Georgine Dyer. She made more money from the shows and movies she did with them than the whole rest of her career put together! It's more than 'a little

52

odd' that one of them should be missing from her photo gallery—it's damned strange. And I think it means something."

"What do you think it means?" he asked.

". . . I don't know yet. But I'll find out."

"Hold on. Remember, all you're supposed to do is keep your eyes and ears open at the studio and fill me in on what's happening."

"Well, of course."

"No snooping and sleuthing on your own."

"Well, of course not. What do you think I am?"

"I plead the fifth on that one. Listen, about our weekend—maybe we can still salvage the rest of it. Can you be ready this evening? I could pick you up about six. Okay?"

Thank God she hadn't returned the granny gown! Of course, she'd pack her new teddy, too—for variety.

There were perhaps forty-five people in the main rehearsal room at the Meyer studios, smoking, drinking coffee or soda, the on-calls engaged in a last-minute study of the day's lines. Nina and Robin Tally sat toward the back. "This had better be good," Nina muttered under her breath as Horst Krueger, flanked by Spence Sprague and Helen Meyer, shuffled some papers and rose to his feet.

"Everybody," he said in a tired voice, "if I may have your attention, please."

The group quickly fell silent. "I come here with a heavy heart this morning," he began. "As you all know, May Minton was found dead in her apartment late yesterday afternoon. Her death is being investigated, which probably means there's reason to believe that she was murdered. In fact," his eyes searched the group, "it was our own Nina McFall who discovered the body."

There was a brief flurry of gasps and buzzing, and some cast members turned to look at Nina, who calmly stared straight ahead, ignoring their unspoken questions. "All of us, of course," Horst went on, "are extremely sorry over the passing of a major talent in the American theater; it strikes those gathered here this morning with a special, most personal impact."

Despite her own sorrow, Nina was irritated by the production Horst was making of things. Crocodile tears. *You're only crying because she put a big kink in your grandiose plans. You're stuck, and you know it.*

The tall, craggy man, his thick mane of black hair slightly grizzled, paused for effect. In his early fifties, he was still lean, imposing, almost handsome, Nina conceded. *There are those of us,* she mused, sending a glance at Angela Dolan, *who think so anyway.*

"And while we extend our deepest sympathies to any and all surviving family members," Horst droned on, "we of *The Turning Seasons* family are confronted with a crisis of our own.

"As you know, May Minton was scheduled to join us Monday morning. She and her long-time colleagues, Sylvia Kastle and Georgine Dyer, were to become temporary members of the TTS cast. They were going to attempt to improve our sagging ratings, to share with us new insights into the will-o'-the-wisp acting business as well. Now that cannot be."

Nina stifled a giggle. *Will-o'-the-wisp? Oh, brother!*

"Normally such a tragedy would have meant scrapping these aggressive plans," he sent a smile at Helen Meyer, "and falling back on previously written scripts, hoping for the best. I suppose that's what a more fainthearted producer would have done . . . eaten his losses.

"But no. I want you to know that Helen, Ken Frost, our writers, and I have been up most of the night revamping the scripts, struggling to come up with a plan to enable us to keep running with the ball." He smiled victoriously. "We think we've done it!"

It was at this point that Nina concentrated on the smugly smiling Helen Meyer. Smartly attired in a gray-green suit neatly edged by the collar and cuffs of a black silk blouse, her platinum hair perfectly coiffed, the fifty-five-year-old woman was almost regal in her bearing. More than that, she was obviously full of herself. Her plans would go forward, death of a major principal or not; she would prevail.

Yes, that was Helen's specialty. Making things happen. And Heaven help anyone who got in her way. Nina winced. That, she knew from personal experience. And while Helen had seemingly mellowed toward Nina after the nightmarish investigation into Morty Meyer's death, Nina still walked very carefully when around Helen. Let sleeping vipers lie. . . .

Even so, as she listened to Horst Krueger drone on, Nina was filled with doubts. How ever would they salvage things this time?

But it was even worse than she'd imagined. Her jaw fell as Horst got to the nut of his speech. "Originally May and her dotty friends were to be evicted from a train passing through Kingston Falls because they hadn't paid their fare. This charming trio of grifters was to have insinuated itself into the town fabric upon being allowed into the Allender home, supposedly for an overnight stay. Sort of a take-off on *The Man Who Came to Dinner*.

"That concept basically holds. The two con-ladies, Sylvia Kastle and Georgine Dyer, will still be kicked off the train in Monday's episode. But instead of being taken in by the gullible Allender family, they will foist themselves upon Harriet Taylor, the town's gossip peddler and chief troublemaker. Who is, of course, Angela Dolan."

Uh-oh. Nina tensed. Here it comes.

"Which means, in essence, that Angela will be absorbing, to a large degree, many of the character quirks that May Minton would have brought to the show. This transition will be done skillfully, of course, so that our viewers will never detect the gradual change in Angela's characterization. We've discussed all this in detail with Angela, and she's graciously agreed to accept this major challenge, to come to our rescue." Here Krueger stopped and sent Angela a sappy grin, which Angela returned in kind.

Nina groaned inwardly. Saint Angela to the rescue? Lordy, as if she isn't hard enough to take now!

"So the main burden of this sweeping face-lift will fall on Angela. There are major script changes throughout, which you are all expected to keep abreast of. There will be a decided change in the show's mood, an injection of whimsy if you will. This too, you *will* all learn to live with, whether you agree with the changes or not."

His voice became stern, dared argument. "These new policies have been carefully thought out and discussed by all members of the board. Though they aren't set in concrete, I wouldn't recommend that anyone try to buck us at this point. We *will* give it a chance. And if at the end of the first week, we see that it's not working, we'll welcome comments at that time. Is that clear?"

There was no response. Everyone stared straight ahead, eyes glazed by the staggering ramifications posed by this shift in show focus, by the idea of Angela the Hun running roughshod over the entire cast.

"Any questions?" Krueger demanded.

Again, numbing silence; the temperature in the rehearsal hall had dropped ten degrees.

"The scripts for Monday are ready, and you'll get your copies right after this meeting. This is another radical departure, I realize, but it serves to emphasize the emergency conditions we're operating under here. Give them a good, hard look over the weekend. Be ready bright and early on Monday to give the new look all you've got."

Some of the actors rose, prepared to leave. "One last thing," Krueger said, his tone settling them again. "And that's your behavior with our newcomers Monday. They'll be confused, perhaps even frightened by the ambience here. It's your job to be patient with them, help them in any way possible. Any open show of hostility, and you'll be duking it out with me, understand? And please, folks, keep a lid on the salty language."

"Sermon over," Nina said to Robin. "Go ye and sin no more."

"Whew!" Robin responded. "What a kick in the head." She made a wry face. "Oh, gag me with a spoon. Will you look at that?"

They turned and took in the cloying scene of Angela, Horst, and Helen gathered in close conclave, smiling and laughing among themselves. Angela Dolan was staring up at Horst, a calf-eyed expression on her face; she clung to his right arm possessively.

To the Howdy-Doody tune, Nina paraphrased, "It's reign-of-terror time."

As they progressed to Myrna Rowan's office to pick up Monday's scripts, Nina felt niggling suspicions—half-humorous, half-serious—skittering through her mind. Had she been set up? That luncheon with Angela—some dirty pool, perhaps, or a brilliant demonstration of reverse English? Had Angela deliberately staged the whole thing, just to throw her off the scent?

Considering the just-finished steamrollering at Krueger's hands, she was almost inclined to go along with Dino's theory. Could it be? Could Angela really have been behind May Minton's murder?

Impossible, she scoffed. Now you *are* going off the deep end. But was she? She had cried "impossible" before, only to have the facts blow up in her face.

For sure, for sure, she concluded. I'll certainly have to keep a close eye on that lady.

Nina returned to her apartment shortly after 1:30 P.M., firmly intending to catch a little nap before stealing a peek at Monday's shooting script. Last night's sleeplessness had left her a trifle logy.

But such was not to be. For she had barely entered her bedroom when the phone rang. Her heart lifted as she recognized Dino's voice.

"I just thought I'd let you know what the ME found out about May Minton. She was dead at least ten minutes before she ever got near that shower. There was no water in her lungs. Severe concussion, a half-inch depression at the base of her skull. The broad who hit her was one tough cookie."

"Broad?" Nina's pulse revved up suddenly.

"Yeah. Jagedorn came up with some alien hair samples in the bathroom. Long, female hair. Blond.

And get this: There were scraps of the same hair in the tub, some caught in Minton's fingernails.''

"A woman?'' Nina puzzled. "I can't believe it. How could a woman do a thing like that? Be strong enough . . . have the guts to do it?''

Rossi almost gloated. "What woman, whom we discussed only yesterday, has blond hair?''

Nina knew a sinking feeling. Still reeling from the morning's experience, she could almost—almost, but not quite—believe it. "So? What are you going to do, ask Angela for a sample of her hair? Or maybe you expect me to get you some?''

"You're reading my mind.''

"And what about the guard at May's apartment building? Does he remember if the woman who went up was a blonde?''

There was momentary silence on the other end of the line. "No,'' Rossi said in a deflated voice. "She had dark brown hair. I checked her out, even talked to her. That's what Charley and I were doing all morning, knocking on doors all over Carson Place.''

"So that blows your theory about Angela, doesn't it?''

"Not really,'' he said, a defensive edge to his voice. "We're still checking out the morning visitors. It's just possible, isn't it, that the murderer might have gotten in earlier and was already with her even while you were talking to her.''

"That's hard to believe. She sounded perfectly normal when I spoke to her. If someone was holding a knife to her throat, I think I'd have detected it. Remember, I knew May fairly well.''

"As I say, it's only an idea. We've got plenty of other doors to pound on before we're done.'' His voice faltered. "Which brings me to another thing.''

"Yes?''

"The trip—it's off.''

"Oh, no! But why?"

"This damned murder. May Minton's still a bigger name than I realized. The press is on it hard. They're making waves all the way up to the IG's office. I'll be working all weekend."

"Oh, darling. I was so counting on our time together. Can't you find some way to get out of it? You've certainly earned some free time."

"That's not how it works, Nina. We get our free time when it's available. When we're chasing burglars, pitch men, penny-ante stuff like that, then we can take some time for ourselves. But murders are an entirely different matter. I'm just as sorry as you are, honey. Peter's going to be crushed. I haven't told him yet. He's still in school."

Nina tried not to be petulant, but she couldn't help herself. "It isn't fair," she protested. "Even policemen need time off. And when we had our hearts so set on it . . ."

"Life isn't always fair. I guess we both know about that."

She choked back disappointment. "Okay. There'll be other times, I know. We've got a couple of weeks before the colors fade. We'll plan again." She paused. "Maybe Peter and I can go to the zoo or something tomorrow afternoon. That might compensate."

"Nina, you're great. I'll pay for any expenses you run up."

"I've got money, Dino. I wish you'd let me . . ."

"*I'll pay*," he said. Nina recognized the edge, backed off.

"I'm sorry, Dino," she sighed contritely, remembering how he felt about being the main provider. "Okay, you pay."

"Damned right," he said, forcing a laugh. "And we *do* have a date for tomorrow night, right? I'll see if I can get some tickets for a show. Something with lots of laughs, lots of music. Okay?''

"Wonderful," she said, chastened. "Whatever you decide will be fine. Tomorrow . . . do you think you could stay the night?''

He chuckled softly. "Yes, I think that can be arranged. Thanks for the suggestion.''

"Anytime, love. Call me tomorrow?''

"Sure thing. What's on for tonight?''

"I'll stay home. Read a book or something. There's an Updike I've been meaning to crack.''

"Okay, Nina. Be sure you do that. No snooping around deserted shopping malls, understand?''

Nina laughed. "I promise. I'm cured, really.''

"Good. You stick to that. Love you. Roger and out.''

Nina decided, since she was sprawled on the bed, to catch the much-needed forty winks. But again she was thwarted by the phone. "Yes?''

"Miss McFall?'' the mellow female voice said. "You don't know me. I got your number from May Minton.''

A mouse ran across Nina's grave. But May Minton was dead!

"Who . . .'' she started, almost dreading the answer, "who's calling, please?''

"As I say, you don't know me. I'm an old friend of May's. My name is Sylvia Kastle.''

Nina released an astonished gasp. "Yes, Miss Kastle. Of course. I was at a loss for a moment there. I—I'm so very sorry about what happened to May. I'm sure that you . . . having known her for so many years . . . must be suffering terribly.''

Sylvia Kastle's voice wavered. "That's what I wanted to talk to you about, Miss McFall. I have to talk to somebody about May. And about the taping that's coming up Monday. May said she was going

61

to talk to you about the inner workings and such. She was then going to pass the information along to me. But, as you can see, she never did learn anything. . . ." Her voice broke.

"Miss Kastle," Nina soothed, "please don't cry. It's going to be all right."

"I hate dreadfully to impose, Miss McFall. But if you could find it in the kindness of your heart to help an old woman in grief . . ."

"Of course, Miss Kastle. What can I do to help?"

"If I could come over for a bit, talk to you. If you'll give me your address . . ."

"Yes, I suppose that would be all right. I'm at Primrose Towers, on Seventy-fourth near Riverside."

"Oh, yes, I know the location."

"When would you like to come?"

"Would right now be convenient? I happen to be in the city. My chauffeur will drive me over; I can be there in twenty minutes. Are you sure I'm not imposing, Miss McFall?"

Nina held the receiver away from her face, gave it a look of disbelief.

"Miss McFall, are you there?"

And away we go, Nina told herself. "Yes, Miss Kastle," she said, struggling to keep the curiosity out of her voice, "that would be just fine. Come right over."

Chapter Five

At sixty-three, Sylvia Kastle was a slender and strikingly attractive woman—years of beauty-salon pampering had seen to that. Though Nina had often seen her in films, on TV reruns and in occasional theater magazines, she was surprised at how much more vital and magnetic she was in the flesh than on film and tape. In fact she was amazed at Kastle's decidedly intimidating *presence*. Why this feeling of awe? she wondered. What sorcery was Kastle employing that so quickly relegated Nina to second-banana status, and in her own apartment at that?

Nina credited the unnatural deference to simple hero worship. After all, Sylvia Kastle, like May Minton, was one of the living legends of the American theater.

Sylvia's complexion was still clear and relatively unlined. There was no sag to her jawline, no wattling around her throat. A small woman, no more than five feet in her stocking feet, her face was a lovely oval, her head crowned by a mass of beautifully coiffed tawny blond hair, for which Nina suspected chemical augmentation was responsible.

Another disconcerting observation: After Sylvia Kastle's teary performance on the phone just thirty

63

minutes earlier, Nina was puzzled to find the woman totally in control—almost remote, actually. Why the sudden turnaround?

Sylvia's surprisingly svelte figure was draped in a clinging, forest-green designer creation adorned by a diamond and sapphire necklace in the shape of a swooping swallow, easily worth fifty thousand dollars, Nina estimated. The neckline was deeply scalloped, the better to display the jewelry as well as Sylvia's still very respectable cleavage. She wore gray stockings and green kid pumps with three-inch heels to compensate for her tiny stature. An exquisite sable scarf completed the ensemble, the total effect being one of fragile royalty, perhaps in exile.

So, Nina thought again, how does Sylvia Kastle project such self-assurance and power? She'd seen overdressed women before—coarse wives of wholesale meat dealers and dress manufacturers—but they hadn't put her off stride the way Sylvia was doing.

Sylvia Kastle had not come empty-handed. A uniformed chauffeur stood behind her in the corridor as Nina opened her door, his arms loaded. Gravely he handed over a two-pound box of Godiva chocolates, a magnum of Mumm's champagne and a container of orange juice. "Don't say a thing," Sylvia shushed when Nina protested. "A little something for allowing me to come on such short notice. Besides, I'm crazy about mimosas. Not an afternoon goes by that I don't indulge." She winked charmingly. "Just to take the edge off things."

And so it was mimosas at 3:30 in the afternoon, an easy enough cocktail to mix up. Sylvia hadn't exaggerated her affinity for the elegant concoction, which had the effect of dissolving her Queen Mother facade very quickly.

Finally there was a break in their warm-up chitchat, after Sylvia had finished her oohing and aah-

64

ing over Nina's apartment. "I want to tell you how sorry I am about May," Nina said. "It must have been a terrible shock."

The woman's face quickly collapsed, and she snatched a lace-edged handkerchief from her bag, dabbing her eyes energetically. Even now, Nina thought, there's a certain stagey quality to her grief. "I've known May for almost thirty-five years," she sobbed, "fifteen of them while she, Georgine, and I were the toast of Hollywood and Broadway. Not once, in all that time, did a cross word pass between us." She stifled more sobs, then collected herself and said, "You were there, Miss McFall. When the police arrived, I mean. What did they find out? Did they mention any possible suspects? Oh, God, if I ever get my hands on the man who murdered her . . ."

"No, Miss Kastle, I didn't hear a thing," Nina said guardedly. She wasn't about to discuss her liaison with Dino Rossi or her special working relationship with his unique squad. "I just had the terrible misfortune to wander in on the awful scene."

Sylvia Kastle leaned forward. "Tell me, Miss McFall," she urged, "just what did things look like there?" Her voice dropped to a sibilant hiss. "Was there any sign that she'd been . . . You know . . . sexually molested? I tell you, the way the world is today, the way some of these men act . . ."

Nina suppressed a grimace. "No, Miss Kastle, there was nothing like that. Not at all."

"Let's knock off this 'Miss' garbage," she said unsteadily—more of her genteel facade was peeling away. "Anyway, it's Mrs.—Mrs. Lance Kirby. He's into real estate, *deeply* into real estate. We've been married forever, it seems. I want you to call me Sylvia, and I'll call you Nina, all right?"

"Fine, Sylvia. Real estate, you say? Just what kind exactly? Homes, buildings, things like that?"

"Lance is in developing. None of that nickel and dime stuff for him. He builds fancy apartment complexes from scratch, tears down the old stuff, puts up spanking new fifty- and sixty-story buildings. It's all very complicated. But no one has to worry about my Lance. He can handle himself in the clinches, all right." Her eyes filled up again. "Now, Nina, tell me more about what happened to poor dear May."

Nina felt squeamish about the turn the conversation was taking. And yet she knew there were ghoulish women like this, who gloried in the seamy details of murder. Whatever turns you on, she mused. Even so, she was still very stingy with graphic details.

"When I came in, she was in the tub, naked," she began grudgingly. "The shower was running full-force. May was lying face-down in the tub. Her hair had clogged the drain. Another five minutes and the water would have overflowed."

"It was rather an unpleasant sight, I suppose."

"It certainly was. I got pretty woozy for a minute or so."

"I imagine. You must be quite a gutsy gal, Nina, to go barging into that bathroom like that, not knowing what you'd find behind that door."

"I don't know if I'd call it gutsy. I was very worried about May, and I wanted to help if I could. I felt uneasy in the lobby when she wasn't answering her phone. So by the time I got upstairs, all I wanted to do was to find May, and fast."

Sylvia made a face. "Lord, I'd have had the shakes so bad . . . You are one brave gal, whether you think so or not. And you say the cops didn't tell you anything?"

"Nothing," Nina said. "Why should they reveal

any inside information to me? To them, I was just an innocent bystander.''

''And they haven't called you back to ask you any additional questions? They didn't let anything slip then?''

''No,'' Nina insisted, becoming irritated at the line of questioning. Why did the woman keep hammering on that point? ''They didn't waste any words. Mostly they were double-checking on why I'd gone to see May in the first place. And they asked if I was on speaking terms with you and Georgine Dyer. Which I could honestly deny—at least until this afternoon.''

''Yes. Life's a real kick, isn't it?'' Sylvia sighed. ''Never can tell what's going to happen next. Like May's death. One minute we're all excited about this soap opera venture, on the phone every spare minute, and the next, it's all over.''

''Not really *all* over, Sylvia. You and Miss Dyer are honoring your commitment, aren't you? We had a meeting just this morning about the shift in plans.''

''I can't speak for Georgine, but I certainly am. If my heart doesn't give out by then. I'm *terrified*.''

''But why? With all your experience, it'll be duck soup.''

''Duck soup, my eye! I've talked to other show people who tried the soaps, and they say it's poison, the hardest work they've ever done. It absolutely put them to the wall.''

''Well, it *is* different, that's for certain,'' Nina admitted. ''The pressure can get to you if you let it. We're putting together a show a day—virtually live— *every* day. Compare that to the old days of live TV, when they spent a week getting ready for just *one* show.''

Sylvia shook her head. ''I'm getting too old for this sort of thing. I wouldn't have done it if May hadn't wheedled me into it. And now she's gone off and left us in the lurch, the old bat." It seemed to Nina that, for the first time, there was sincere affection in Sylvia Kastle's voice.

"Just don't panic," she advised. "Take it five minutes at a time. If you think about the whole day's schedule, it'll send you running for the nearest exit."

Sylvia took a strong pull at her mimosa, almost as if drinking courage. "Tell me how a typical day goes."

Nina described the 8:00 A.M. call and the progression of rehearsals, stopping often to outline the routines involved in each.

"And by three o'clock we're free to leave?" Sylvia asked hopefully.

"After a fashion. Usually we wait around while the tape rolls a second time, just in case we've got a boom shadow or someone standing in the background who shouldn't be there. That's rare, but it can happen. Then it's a scene retake, and Spence really blows his stack, overtime rates being what they are."

"And after that?"

"You pick up the next day's script and go home. Where you collapse, grab a bite, then start learning new lines all over again. You're usually in bed by ten or eleven so you can be up by six to make your eight A.M. call. Doesn't that sound romantic and exciting?"

Sylvia's face was incredulous. "And you do this every day of the week?"

"No. Some days you're written out of the script. Today and yesterday, I wasn't in any scenes, so I got a couple days off." Nina frowned. "It wasn't what I'd call a fun time. Now *this* weekend—like you—I've got sixty pages staring me in the face for

68

the Monday call. Thank goodness they aren't all mine.''

''Oh, Nina, now I *am* frightened. I'll never be able to stand up to that!''

Nina laughed. ''You just think you won't. Once you're on the set, with a good director behind you and a competent cast to work with, it'll be like the old days. You'll forget you were ever away.''

''I hope you're right.''

''I'll be there to help you; we'll all be there. Spence and the other directors will handle you with kid gloves—the first few days, anyway. After that it's dog-eat-dog.''

''I've already skimmed my script. They delivered it to me this morning. It's really funny. And this woman who's sort of assuming May's lines—Angela Dolan, I think. How is she?''

''Angela's an old pro. She's the main anchor. Been around since Edison invented the movie camera.''

''I mean, what kind of a person is she?''

''You'll have to decide that for yourself, Sylvia. One thing: don't blink or she'll steal your scene just like that.''

Sylvia grimaced. ''Oh, one of those. May was good at that, too. Upstaged you at the drop of a hat. Thanks for the warning.''

''It's not a warning. Some people take to Angela—'' Nina paused ''—some don't. Enough said.''

Sylvia held up her glass. ''Do you suppose, Nina, I might have one more? Then I must be going. I hadn't intended to stay this long—goodness, it's almost five—but this has all been so interesting.''

She struggled to her feet, weaved to Nina's phone. ''I'll just call Genno's little hangout, have him start out. By the time he gets here I'll be done with my drinkie.''

But "almost five" or not, Sylvia Kastle wasn't really ready to leave. Somehow the conversation looped back on itself, and Nina found herself being regaled with endless tales of yesteryear in Tinsel Town.

". . . And so there was May," Sylvia Kastle wheezed, almost convulsed with laughter, ". . . alone with Edgar Hodges. He was one of Hollywood's biggest directors during the fifties. But she didn't want to be there, because she was interested in Allan Dixon, who was her leading man and a real dreamboat. We had to think of a way to rescue her from old Edgar.

"It was Georgine who put on that sound-effects record in the living room—a police car siren. She turned it up full-blast, then went knocking on the door. 'There are some police officers coming up the walk,' she yelled. 'I think you two should get dressed, fast.'

"Well, Edgar Hodges was in the middle of a messy divorce at the time, and he was supposed to be keeping his nose clean. He came out of that room like a shot, hit the hall running and streaked out the back door. The next morning we found his shoes on the street where his car had been parked."

Nina laughed dutifully, wondering if it was a case of "you had to be there." Sylvia plunged on as though this relatively mild incident was the raciest thing Hollywood had ever witnessed.

"Well, we finally located Dixon and he came over. Brought a couple of pals along, and we danced till dawn." Sylvia winked at Nina. "I really shouldn't be telling you all this. You must think I'm *awful*. But that's the way things were in those days. We had some marvelous times." She stared into space, a contradictory twinge of sadness reflected in her gaze.

"But all that changed when Tucker O'Brien came on the scene."

Nina's ears perked up. "Tucker O'Brien? He was the director who started casting all three of you together, wasn't he?"

"That's right. It was the saddest day of my life when he died. I was in love with that man. Or at least I thought I was. We all thought we were, for a while." She lapsed into silence.

"What can you tell me about his murder, Sylvia?" Nina pressed, ashamed of herself for taking advantage of the older woman's condition, but determined just the same. "It was so strange, the way everything got all hushed up so fast. It was almost like a conspiracy. I read a book a while back—*A Cast of Killers*, it was called—and it dealt with the murder of a famous Hollywood director back in the twenties. The studio, the police, his friends all worked to hide the murderer. It reminds me of your friend, Tucker. Can you let me in on what really happened, Sylvia?"

"Oh, sure," the woman started glibly, "only I wouldn't think anybody'd still be interested in ancient history like that. I remember it like it was yesterday."

At that moment the telephone jangled. *Damnation*, Nina groaned inwardly. Of all times for the phone to ring!

"There's a limousine here for a Mrs. Kirby," the doorman said. "The chauffeur says he's been waiting some time."

"Tell him she'll be right down." Forcing a smile, Nina turned back to her guest. "This has been so much fun, Sylvia," she said. "We'll have to do it again sometime."

"Yes," Sylvia said. "We must."

Then she was leaving Nina's apartment, strug-

71

gling to arrange her sable scarf as she went. She waved tipsily at Nina just before she went out the door. "See you Monday bright and early, dear. And thanks ever so much. You've been such a *marvelous* help."

For long moments after the woman left, Nina sat staring into space, turning the bowl of her glass carefully in her fingers, sipping at the dregs of her momosa, even though she didn't want it. *And what do we have here? Just wait until I dangle some of these strings before Dino tomorrow night.*

Still, something nagged at her, an indefinable inconsistency she couldn't quite pin down. Sylvia Kastle had purportedly come to visit because she wanted to talk about May Minton and about her upcoming stint on *The Turning Seasons*. And yes, they had talked about May and the TTS routines. But something rang hollow. What, exactly, had been Sylvia Kastle's underlying purpose in coming? Hadn't her insistence on knowing the details of her best friend's murder been just the least bit morbid?

Nina credited her muzzy thinking to the champagne. It would come, she told herself, give it time. And when it did . . .

Strange woman, she thought, picking up the phone. *Very strange indeed.*

"Lincoln Center Library for the Performing Arts. May I help you?"

"Yes, please. How late are you open today?"

Chapter Six

On Saturday morning, Nina took Peter to the Metropolitan Museum of Art as a way of compensating for the wrecked weekend plans. That evening, Dino splurged on dinner at Le Cirque, then the theater. Rossi was as good as his word, and "Me and My Girl" gave them the lift they needed. (Nina had seen it before, but kept that small fact to herself.)

Now, at 11:10 P.M., back at her apartment, with Dino nursing a scotch on the rocks, Nina refectively sipped a tiny Drambuie.

Wind-down time.

Dino had removed his jacket and loosened his tie, the move serving to display his massive shoulders and muscular chest to advantage. Nina had kicked off her black silk pumps, which lay in the middle of the floor, a subtle reminder of their comfortable intimacy and delights to come.

"Thanks for a marvelous evening, darling," Nina said, nuzzling his throat with her lips. "I just loved the show. Those songs won't stop buzzing through my head. But you know what the best part of this whole evening is? Not the dinner, not the flashy show. It's right here and now—just you and me. As Mr. Wordsworth put it, 'The world is too much with us. Late and soon, getting and spending, we lay waste our powers . . .' ''

Dino's eyes shone with admiration. ''I love it when you do that,'' he said. ''There's no end to your talents.''

Nina squirmed inwardly, basking in the words of praise. ''Stick around for the encore,'' she said, putting on her brassy Streisand voice. ''I'll give you the prologue to *The Canterbury Tales*. You should hear my 'Little Boy Blue,' by Eugene Fields. *That'll* dilute your scotch.'' She immediately launched into the tear-jerking doggerel: '' 'The little toy dog is covered with dust, but sturdy and staunch he stands . . .' ''

''Enough!'' Dino laughed, putting a gentle finger over her lips. ''See why I never compliment you, girl? The eternal schoolteacher. You never know when to quit.''

She effected an exaggerated pout. ''If you weren't so stingy with your kind words, I wouldn't get carried away.''

''Carried *out* is what you're gonna get.''

''Promises, promises.'' She laughed and kissed him again, this time on the end of his nose. The sudden slide of his lips on the smooth flesh of her throat sent burning streamers streaking down her body. ''Honey, don't. . .'' she sighed. ''Unless you're looking for early fireworks.'' Her eyes went sultry. ''I thought we'd have a chance to talk a little before . . . I mean . . .''

''I'm shocked, Nina. Shocked beyond words. Is that all you have on your mind? Say yes.''

''Yes, oh yes.'' She slid silky, restless fingers inside his shirt to caress his hairy chest. ''And aren't you glad? Say yes.''

''Yes, that I am.''

"Thanks, darling, for our night together. I needed it badly."

"But it's not all you have on your mind, is it?"

"No, of course not."

"Well, at least we got through dinner without talking about it."

She smiled at him ruefully. "But we were thinking about it, weren't we?"

"Yeah, we were thinking about it." He stood up and wandered over to the window, gazing out over the Hudson. "Any more ideas about the missing photograph?"

"No answers, really, but maybe a few more pieces of the puzzle." She told him about the peculiar visit from Sylvia Kastle, ending with her evening trip to the library.

"Why did you go there? You must have been worn out."

"I was, but I had to try to find out something."

"Nina, you promised me you'd stick to observing what goes on at the studio. Now you tell me you've gone off by yourself to—"

"To the library. I honestly didn't think I'd need your permission to do something as exotic and dangerous as sit in a library reading thirty-year-old newspapers and magazines."

They glared each other down, the mood of only moments before vanished. She outwaited him.

"All right, what did you find out?"

"Do you really want to know?"

"Don't push it."

She knew he was right. Damn, she always went one step too far. "Well, it was worth the time. I realized that in addition to not having a picture of Sylvia Kastle in her gallery, May never mentioned either her name or Georgine Dyer's. Oh, I brought them up a few times, but she always managed to change the subject. It didn't seem strange then, but now it bothers the hell out of me. Unless there was bad blood between them somewhere in the past, why would she do that?"

"Search me. What did you find at the library?"

"Just this: May Minton, Sylvia Kastle, and Georgine Dyer may have been three of the best actresses ever to put on makeup, but they were also three of the most incorrigible hell-raisers who ever hit Hollywood. They did things the press had to soft-pedal."

"Like what?" Rossi returned to the sofa, intent on what she was telling him.

"Like being involved in a series of really lurid love affairs and divorce triangles. They always seemed to wind up the injured parties in the end, but the trail was definitely smelly. Did you ever hear of the Michael Reardon case?"

"The one where the actor was murdered by his mistress?"

"Yes. May was mixed up in that somehow. The mistress went to jail for it and Reardon's wife went to the funny farm for a while, but I think May was the instigator."

"Why?"

"Not because there was any solid proof, but because that was about the tenth or twelfth sensational trial where her name came up. I'm not too high on coincidences even in small doses, but this was over the rainbow."

"What about Kastle and Dyer?"

"The same sort of thing, but on a lesser scale. And several times their names were mixed up in the same cases as May Minton's. Don't you think it means something?"

"Definitely. It means your power of imagination is exceeded only by your skill in library research."

76

Nina supressed the urge to argue the point. What was the use? Dino wanted solid proof, and all she had were nagging hunches and nasty possibilities. Better to let it all simmer for a while. Sooner or later, something would bubble to the top. Besides, there was that romantic mood to recapture.

"You're probably right, hawkshaw," she said. "In any case, I just can't wait to see Angela in action come Monday. She'll be playing Lady Bountiful all over the place."

"You worry too much." He sank back onto the sofa next to her and ran idle fingers up and down her back, savoring the way her dress slid on the silk of her slip and savoring the touch of his fingertips on the velvet texture of her skin as well.

Nina shivered, gently trapped his hands and held them still. Just one more point before he drove her over the brink. "You really think it's possible that Angela might have done in poor May just to steal her role?"

"It's highly possible. Murderers are usually motivated by basic things like fear, jealousy, rage. A single emotion sets them off. I'll stick with fear, the fact that Angela was frightened by the career threat that May Minton posed. So far we've got nothing else to go on—aside from your so-called hunches. It was a rush job, that's for sure, done in extreme panic. That's Angela's speed, I'd say. And get this. We did some hour-by-hour checking on Angela Dolan on Thursday, and she *wasn't* at the studio that day. You must have gotten your wires crossed, baby. She was written out. She had the day off just like you did—only she put her time to more active use. If you follow me."

Nina jerked away, sat upright. To hell with the mood—for now. "Are you positive? I could have sworn she was in the script on Thursday."

"We're sure. So, understandably, Ms. Dolan is still number one on our hit parade. We don't have anything solid yet, but we're digging. We're still trying to figure out how she got into that building. No angles so far, but we'll get there. We're temporarily holding off bringing her in for questioning. We don't want to spook the lady before we get our ducks lined up."

"And what did you find out? Was Angela anywhere near Carson Place that day?"

"We've got nothing solid yet. In fact we don't even know where she was on Thursday. We assigned a car to sit on her immediately, but she never came home until after midnight. Mighty late hours for a soaper queen with an eight o'clock call the next morning, wouldn't you say?"

"Maybe I'll save you some time, ask her point blank. 'Where were you all day Thursday, Angela?' Good idea?"

Dino's eyes turned angry. "Let us handle it our own way, Miss Fix-it."

Nina shook her head. "I still don't buy it, Dino. I just don't see Angela having the guts to do a thing like that, to bash in someone's skull. By the way, any sign of the murder weapon yet?"

"None. She must have brought it along and taken it away with her. Or else she used something she found in the apartment and she lifted it. From the profile of the dent in the head, it was something shaped like a piece of pipe. A blackjack? Hardly the kind of thing you'd find in a woman's bag. Which is not to say she couldn't have purchased something special. We're checking that too."

"Dino, this is sounding more ridiculous by the minute. I know Angela, and I just don't believe she's capable of such a thing, even if she did have a motive."

"Nice to know you realize she had one."

"Lots of people could have had motives. I'll give you a scenario with a suspect and a motive grounded in solid fact, but just as unlikely as your Dolan fantasy."

"Go on." She really had his attention now—hard facts did it for this man, every time.

"Picture a young actor struggling to make a name for himself. He's good-looking and talented, but he's totally unknown. No agents, no contacts, no luck. Nothing but hope, and that's dwindling fast."

"I get the general idea. Continue."

"One day, shazam! He gets lucky. A famous actress sees his photograph, locates him, and calls him to do an audition. It's a small part, but it has one good scene. It's what every young actor dreams about—a chance to be seen."

"This famous actress wouldn't have the initials MM, would she? And I don't mean Marilyn Monroe."

"You're really paying attention, aren't you? I like that. Well, he gets the part and the show goes into rehearsal. Things are really looking up for this fellow, and he dares to dream about success. He even begins to hope that he'll be able to afford to get married soon—there's a sweet young thing in the background . . ."

"Isn't there always?"

" . . . and they've been engaged for several months. She's an actress too, or at least trying to be. They both know that if he can just get a foot in the door, he'll be able to help her career along as well."

"How many handkerchiefs am I going to need for this?"

"Shut up. This is true, it really happened. One day, about two weeks into rehearsal, he thinks he's getting the come-on from the leading lady. Impossible, he tells himself; she's a big glamorous star and he's a little nobody. But it keeps happening, and it's hard to ignore. Finally he gets the direct approach—she lets him know she needs an 'escort' for a dinner party. He says he doesn't have a dinner jacket. She offers to buy one for him. And everything that goes along with it.''

"Have you seen *Sunset Boulevard* lately?"

"I know, but this is where the similarities end. Our young man politely, gently, and naively tells the star about his fiancée. Remember, this was several decades ago, in the days where nice young men were still nice young men. At least this one was. So the roof falls in and before he knows what's happened, he's out on the street, replaced by another actor.''

"Isn't that kind of thing illegal?"

"Sure. If it can be proved. There was a medium-sized stink, and a hearing was held. It got a fair amount of press. But who'd be believed, an established star or an unknown actor?"

"What happened?"

"The play opened to raves and had a long run. The replacement was noticed and went on to a wonderful Broadway career.''

"And our young hero?"

"He struggled some more, got a slow start, gradually became known as a reliable supporting player, and finally married his fiancée. She became pregnant and retired from show business to devote herself to home and family. Their kids grew up and married. They had grandchildren, and she died a few years ago, without ever returning to her career. He's still working as an actor.''

"So May Minton has someone besides Angela Dolan sore at her. That's a long story for such a small point.''

80

"The point is that 'our hero' is working on TTS. His name is Noel Winston. And don't bother to ask, I can tell you, he wasn't on call the day of the murder, either. So, do you want to book him now, or should we wait until the morning?"

"I know you're being cute and pretending to finger another one of your pals to make a point, but I have to tell you you've raised a serious possibility."

"What!"

"Sure. People nurse grudges for years. Maybe Winston kept it under control as long as he didn't come into contact with her, but then the prospect of having to work with her set him off."

"How can you *say* such a thing? I told you all that to make you see how farfetched facts can be. Every word is absolute truth—I found it in the library along with other stuff. But the conclusion is Loony Tunes and Merry Melodies. You have to see that! Noel is an absolute lamb—he wouldn't hurt a fly!"

"Nina, I understand how strongly you're influenced by your feelings. But I can't work that way. I deal in facts, and facts don't have feelings."

"I wonder sometimes if *you* have feelings." A hard silence set in while he sat there and sipped his scotch and she bit her nails, thinking of a way to unsay it. She began softly. "Dino, I'm sorry. That was a stupid thing to say. It came out of sheer frustration, and I know you know I didn't mean it." Over to him.

"By the way, thanks for taking Peter out today. He told me he had a great time. He said he never knew art museums could be so much fun. How did you manage that?"

She shot him an impish smile, recognizing that the change of subject was his way of accepting her apology. How well they were getting to know each other!

"No problem. I have him the McFall special—steered him toward the Van Goghs and told him how the artist flipped out, cut his ear off and gave it to his girlfriend."

"Hey, who said art is stuffy?"

"Then we went to look at the Gauguins. I think Peter has a thing about Pacific Islands. Or maybe it's all those boobs on the Gauguin models. He got big eyes a few times there."

"You fruitloop!"

"Beyond that, I think he was really impressed by being with a celebrity. Maybe now he'll take me for real."

"A celebrity?"

"People kept recognizing me in the museum—a few even asked me for autographs. Peter got a little puffed up over that, I think."

"Sounds like my boy. How did he behave?"

"He was just fine. A bit smarty-pants at times—you know how kids are. They can be so condescending when they think you don't dig Michael J. Fox or Mötley Crüe. But I hung in there. No, there's nothing wrong with Peter that spending a little more time with his father wouldn't help."

"Now it's guilt-trip time, huh?"

"If the shoe fits, darling. He *does* idolize you." Her voice became wistful. "Don't let that get away from you, too."

"You're right." He deliberately ignored the small feint. "I've just got to do it."

She let it rest there—leave well enough alone. For the moment, she was content to cuddle in his arms, thinking her own thoughts.

Which, of course, revolved around him. Just where, she mused, was their relationship going? They had met in June, and in October they were still drifting. Was there a future at all for them? Was marriage on her agenda? Hardly. At least not now, not until some basic issues were settled between them. Foremost was the matter of her career. Could she possibly toss over this job she loved so much— and the fabulous salary that went with it—to be Mrs. Rossi, just to soothe his monstrous ego? To cater to his Neanderthal me-Tarzan, you-Jane idea of the way a marriage should go?

But you love Dino, she argued, you know you do. Your life would be a shambles without him. And Dino loves you, even though he sometimes acts as though telling you about it is a violation of national security restrictions. But he *has* told you, and you know there's nobody else in the picture, not for Dino. The original one-woman man; they broke the mold after they made him.

So why the jitters? You know what he's like. Marry him and you'll be surrendering all your beautiful independence. He'll be the boss, possessive and domineering; you'll be the meek little wife, privileged to exist in his shadow. Are you ready to trade your *glitterati* lifestyle for that?

Nina stifled a laugh. Big deal. All this commotion, when what it all boils down to is the fact that not once, in all these months, has Dino said the first word about marriage. When he does, then, perhaps, it will be time to start fretting.

But he won't, she sighed, her thoughts coming full circle. And not just because his first marriage had fizzled, either. That old-world stubbornness and pride again. His macho pigheadedness where her income was concerned.

"A penny for your thoughts," Dino interrupted, tilting her chin up with his fingers, smiling gently down at her.

"A thousand bucks wouldn't even begin to put a

dent in what I'm thinking," she said, her smile forced.

"That bad? I thought we were having a nice time."

"We were. We *are*."

She lifted her face to Dino's, her eyes blurring with emotion. "Where were we," she murmured, "when we were so rudely interrupted?"

The invitation could not be easily refused. Dino's handsome face drifted down, a smile on his sensuous lips.

Chapter Seven

On Sunday, Nina and Dino seemed to have a tacit agreement to steer clear of any discussion of the Minton murder. The pact was put to the acid test when Nina opened the Sunday paper and found several pages of copy and many photographs reviewing May's career as one of the most beloved stars of the . . . blah blah blah. She read it all in silence; there was nothing there she hadn't already learned, and she was able to distinguish the facts from the fluff.

When she finished, she left the section of the paper folded open to the murder coverage and wordlessly set it beside Dino. Later, she saw him pick it up and scan it thoroughly, also without comment.

Better to spend the day like an ordinary couple enjoying a leisurely Sunday, Nina thought. And so they did, although the words *ordinary* and *leisurely* bore little resemblance to the scene in the McFall apartment.

Late in the afternoon there was a terrific thunderstorm and an intense cloudburst that set records. Nina and Dino didn't notice; they were busy setting a few records of their own.

Not until she was on her way to the studio Monday
morning for the 8:00 A.M. call did Nina allow herself
to think about the case. Not consciously, that is. And
even then she had one overriding thought—the reali-
zation that she was burning to meet Georgine Dyer.

At the rehearsal hall in Meyer Studios, the order
of the day was tension. Monday mornings were
never anybody's favorite time of the week, but this
day was exceptional.

Nina lost no time in finding Georgine Dyer. She
was sitting over to one side, alone, apparently
watching Sylvia Kastle and Angela Dolan Alphonse-
and-Gaston each other to a fare-thee-well. Georgine
was a taller woman than Nina had expected, and
seemed very reserved. Nina thought it odd that no
one was talking to her. Standard TTS behavior was
to do everything possible to make newcomers feel
relaxed and welcome. After all, everyone's performance affected everyone else's, and even one overly
nervous or shaky individual could pull them all
down a few pegs.

Nina observed her quarry for a few moments before approaching. Georgine Dyer, at 61, could have
passed for 51 or 71. She was almost nondescript in
her appearance; everything about her was unexcep-
tional. Mousy-colored hair, cut short and not so
much coiffed as combed. Drab skin with little makeup. Clothing that would have looked appropriate on
a woman doing her grocery shopping. No jewelry.
Neat figure, but nothing out of the ordinary. All in
all, Nina thought Georgine Dyer the most untheat-
rical figure she'd ever seen, and wondered how
she'd ever held her own with the vivacious May
Minton and the elegant Sylvia Kastle.

"Miss Dyer?"

The woman looked up, but said nothing.

"I'm Nina McFall. Melanie Prescott in the script? So glad to meet you."

"How do you do." It was definitely not a question.

"Please allow me to express my sympathy about Miss Minton."

The woman's eyes returned to the Kastle-Dolan skirmishing, but she gave no response beyond a small nod.

Nina persevered. "During the last few months, I was rather friendly with May, and I gather from the things she said that you must feel her loss very keenly. I just want you to know that—"

"May Minton never said any such thing, and you have no idea how I feel about her death. Just what do you want?"

Nina was flabbergasted at the woman's attitude and went into a fast backstroke. "You're absolutely right. I apologize for the clumsy fib. As a matter of fact, May barely even mentioned you or Sylvia Kastle, which seemed strange but who was I to ask questions? I really did get to know her, by the way— that part was true. And I liked her quite a lot. Actually, I only intended to say 'hello,' since we'll be working together for a few weeks, and welcome you to the set."

"Thanks, but you don't have to bother. All I want to do is find out what's expected of me, do it, and get the hell out of here." She looked up abruptly, directly into Nina's eyes, as though to study the effect she'd made. "You can tell me one thing, though."

Nina found her voice. "Yes?"

"Where's the ladies' room?"

Nina watched the woman's figure as she walked silently across the rehearsal hall and disappeared

down a corridor. No one looked up as she passed—
it was as though she wasn't there.

This was one of the legends of the theater? This
brown-paper-bag number? Where was the glamour
of the stage? The mystique of the screen? Where
were the suave manner and cultured attitude that
were supposed to be part of stardom? If this was a
real actress, Nina thought, give me a brass-plated
phony any time.

Nina's thoughts were interrupted as the line rehearsal began, and she didn't see Georgine Dyer
again until her first lines came up in the script. Then
came another revelation: the woman was hysteri-
cally funny! Even in the first read-through, a real
character instantly emerged that had the entire cast
in stitches every time she opened her mouth.

Nina's eyes swerved from Georgine to Sylvia to
Angela and back again. Georgine seemed totally un-
interested in the commotion that ensued after her
every line. Sylvia looked grim, but not surprised. As
for Angela, she looked as though she'd just discovered her rowboat was sinking fast.

After the line rehearsal, they broke up into groups
for blocking on individual scenes. In one group,
Robin Tally as Buffy Kingston and Rafe Fallone as
Dan Marshall were deeply into their thing. And
though the teleprompter rolled steadily, neither
principal—accomplished pros that they were—gave
it any notice. Watching Nick Galano as he sat
hunched over his monitor, Nina and Sylvia Kastle
listened to the assistant director's nonstop drone.

Off to one side, Jill Carstairs, the production assistant, clicked her stopwatch as each line was delivered, making small notations in the margins of her
script. Apparently they were on the nose, for Jill's
expression was relatively serene.

"Amazing," Sylvia Kastle murmured at Nina's

elbow. "I'd forgotten what an art there was to producing a half hour on television. And every day of the week. How do you do it?"

"Routine," Nina said. "I didn't get a decent night's sleep for the first three months after I signed on. But now, it's second nature."

"I'm still terrified of this afternoon," Sylvia Kastle said. "That final take. You mean they absolutely do not stop for anything? Suppose I blow my lines completely?"

"Spence will go on and call for a retake later on, when the whole taping's finished. But it's highly unlikely that a pro like you would freeze. He ignores minor glitches. He figures people will think it was *supposed* to be that way. Retakes and editing can be dreadfully expensive. That's why we have all these endless run-throughs—to avoid such catastrophes in the first place."

"Anyway, I'm still terrified."

"Don't be. We're all pleased and honored to have you on board. I think those opening scenes of yours were a riot."

"Riot, perhaps, but let's be honest. Georgine's stealing this thing out from under me. From under all of us."

"Sylvia, that's not true. She's—"

"It's true, all right. It's always been that way. When I think of the times she's done this to me, I could kill her!"

No, you couldn't, Nina thought. You really couldn't—could you?

"I noticed you trying to get chummy with Georgine this morning," Sylvia said. "Don't waste your energy."

"You mean she's always like that?"

"Oh no, not always. Sometimes she's quite different. This is one of her pleasant days."

"I don't understand. I thought you and Georgine and May were, well, sort of latter-day three musketeers. Pals offstage as well as on."

Sylvia's look of disdain laid that one to rest. "Maybe it was that way once upon a time, but no more. Ever since we each retired, Georgine acts as though she wishes she'd never met us. But why waste time on such a dowdy frump? Even if she can come up with some good line-readings," she added in grudging admiration. "Nina, I hope you've forgiven me for Friday afternoon. Me and my damned mimosas. I'll never learn. The things I must have told you . . ."

"There's nothing to forgive," Nina said. "If a couple of dream-factory debutantes can't let their hair down once in a while, who can?"

"I just don't want you getting the wrong impression. We all have our little lapses, but normally one doesn't go revealing them to perfect strangers."

Nina smiled. "My lips are sealed. I was only sorry that our time was so short. I *am* interested in period stuff like that. I would have liked to know more about your career—and the Tucker O'Brien story. His murder mystifies me."

Did Sylvia withdraw just then, pull down the shutters once more? "And me as well," she said. "It was just one of those things." She looked up, saw someone beckoning her from halfway down the row of half sets. "Oh, there's my call. Wish me luck."

Nina stood watching Sylvia teeter on her three-inch heels through the mess of camera cables. Does she think I'm still an ingenue? she wondered. That Sphinx act of hers every time I press for details about the Tucker O'Brien murder gets old in a big hurry.

* * *

The day had passed with amazing speed. Suddenly it was 2:10; with the dress rehearsal just concluded and last-minute preparations for final tape underway, there were a precious few minutes of breathing space. Coming into the main rehearsal hall for a cold drink, Nina found Georgine Dyer sitting alone on a bench near the soda machine, deep in thought.

"Well, Miss Dyer," she greeted. "How's it going? You look bushed."

"I am. I'm exhausted. How you people can do this day in and day out, I'll never know." She seemed in a somewhat more communicative frame of mind at the moment.

"We don't. Some days we're written out of the script. Without that we couldn't possibly make it. Sorry I can't offer that consolation to you this week. You're very heavy all week. Which is to be expected, since Helen and Horst want to establish you and Miss Kastle as fast as possible."

"Very heavy?" She sent Nina a puzzled look.

"What that means, is that you're written into every scene. Or, in your case, lots of scenes, *every* day."

"So I'm discovering. I don't know if I'm going to be able to keep up the pace." Georgine fanned herself with a discarded script cover. "I'm beginning to question my sanity . . . for ever agreeing to do this damn thing in the first place."

"Why did you?" Nina blurted it out without thinking.

She was rewarded with a sharp look. "Don't worry. I know, from past experience, the consequences of reneging on a contract. I'll go through with it."

Nina decided to take a gamble. "You know, all weekend I've been thinking that things here were

91

going to be impossible today. I mean, having to change everything so abruptly, and all.''

''No, all weekend you were thinking how you could get me to talk about the past. Forget it. You can't.'' And with that, Georgine Dyer stood up and quickly walked away.

A moment later she stopped in her tracks, wheeled around, and came back to the bench. ''Why are you so nosy? Nobody else is.''

''All right, I'll tell you. I'm obsessed with an unsolved mystery—the murder of Tucker O'Brien, and . . .''

''I can save you some time.''

''You can? How?''

''By telling you the truth: I don't know who did it. Tucker's dead and buried. Leave him there. Now scram, I have to study these damn lines.''

And Georgine buried her nose in her script. Clearly, Nina would get no more out of her. But she was aware that Georgine knew her lines backwards and forwards, and had no need to escape into the script. There was more gold to be mined there, she was certain.

Chapter Eight

Nina wasn't heavy at all on Tuesday. In fact, she had only one scene the whole day. As a result, she found herself with time on her hands. Sitting in her dressing room at 10:00 A.M. with the door closed, she was supposedly fine-tuning her lines.

In reality, her mind was light years away from thoughts about what motivated Melanie Prescott, her TTS alter ego.

And though she'd promised herself faithfully that she wouldn't get involved this time, again she mulled murder.

Was Georgine Dyer on the level? Or had she merely been toying with her? Her icy attitude about May—could it possibly be genuine?

And all those scandals the papers had reported so long ago—press agents working overtime? The May Minton she'd known was warm and kind and funny. Not once had she ever exhibited any trace of meanness, any display of temper. Those afternoons with her had been therapeutic, and Nina came away refreshed, on good terms with the world. May was not the kind to dwell on bygone days to maudlin excess. In fact, those times when Nina steered their talk to her career, May had been pleasant enough, charming her with accounts of plays she'd starred in, places she'd visited, interesting celebrities she'd met. But not once had she ever divulged anything the least bit personal in her past. Certainly nothing so sordid as the events Nina had found in the library files, or the things Sylvia had told her. Or whatever it was Georgine wouldn't tell her.

Again and again Nina tried getting her head around the day's shooting script, around the sly machinations the writers had dreamed up for Ms. Prescott, powerhouse female business exec. But she was only good for a few lines. Then images of May Minton floated back.

And how about her hypothesis about May Minton having enemies Nina couldn't even begin to imagine? Could this new information color that?

But definitely. For if May had behaved so badly that Georgine wouldn't even talk about her, or if she were the nympho that Kastle had so graphically described, then there had to be dozens of victims in her past—abused, helpless people whom Minton had trampled along the way to stardom—though Nina found it hard to believe. And shouldn't she—no, Dino—be taking this new disclosure into consideration in his search for May's killer?

Another line of conjecture bobbed to the surface of her mind then, something that had come to her just before dawn, as she'd tossed restlessly in bed. What about *The Turning Seasons'* competitors? What about the other networks with soap operas of their own? Possibly word of Meyer Productions' blockbuster concept had leaked into the grapevine. Wasn't it possible that they'd try to get in on the action, too, head TTS off at the pass?

And if their barracuda reps had approached and been turned down by Minton, was it so utterly impossible to believe that they might have toyed with the idea of a discreet murder in hope of nipping the project in the bud?

Of course it was! It was totally out of the question. Still . . . maybe it *was* something worth mentioning to Rossi, anyway.

Then another thought jangled her interior phone lines. The Tucker O'Brien murder was definitely a strong element here, and there was every reason to believe it *could* reflect upon May's death. Now whom did Nina know who might have a handle on old gossip that had never made its way into the papers? An ex-reporter who'd worked on one of the more gamy New York tabloids of the time, perhaps? Nobody came to mind immediately.

Make a note, Nina. Nose around the studio, see who knows somebody like that. Noel Winston, she thought. He goes back a century or so. He might know just the man.

And failing that, she could always go back to the library. They kept whole walls of microfiches there—you could go blind reading vintage newspapers. It was worth a try. Tomorrow. She was written out of the script; she just might pay the stacks another visit. But in the meantime . . .

She glanced at her watch, saw that she still had ten minutes before her call. I'd better call Dino, she concluded, bounce a few of these things off him. She rose, locked her dressing room door and started toward the pay phone at the end of the hall.

"Nina," Rossi said upon recognizing her voice, "good thing you called. I was going to try you later this afternoon—thought you should be the first to know. We're bringing in Angela Dolan for questioning."

Damnation! Nina thought. But she kept her irritation hidden. "Are you sure that's wise?"

"I'm sure," he said. "We haven't asked her point-blank yet, but we can't establish any alibi for last Thursday afternoon or evening. Can't get a fix on her anywhere. That plus the blond hair we found under Miss Minton's fingernails justifies a little polite questioning. We'll bring in a couple of other cast members, make like it's a general sweep. She shouldn't throw a fit over that."

"Fit? Not at all. Most likely she'll just have her lawyer contact you and read you the riot act. I don't know the ins and outs of this, slander laws being what they are, but I'd say you're skating on some pretty thin ice."

"You got any better ideas?"

"As a matter of fact, I do." And with that, Nina proceeded to fill him in on the things she'd discovered since she'd last seen him, things like her introduction to the sunny Georgine Dyer. "I'd say that Miss Dyer deserves more than casual scrutiny. If May could provoke such intense dislike, she must have done something really despicable once."

"But there's nothing there to prove."

"Can you prove your suspicions about Angela?"

"Not yet, but just give us some time. We'll—"

"The Tucker O'Brien thing stinks to high heaven. The way they all freeze whenever I bring up his murder—spooky. If that isn't a lead, I'll eat it. Maybe you should call in Georgine and Sylvia, too, when you do that sweep of yours. Ask them about Tucker. I have a hunch about that."

Rossi laughed. "One of your hunches, huh? Here we go again!"

"Don't knock it. They worked before, didn't they?"

"They sure did, damn it. That's what eats me.

But it's not the most professional approach to police work, you know."

"Am I asking you to violate police procedures? I'm just suggesting that you pull that Tucker O'Brien file, read it an inch at a time. *That's* professional. You can get your hands on it, can't you?"

"I suppose. It'll take some digging, all the way back to nineteen seventy-two, but it can be done. I just don't see the need, honestly, when we already have a rock-solid lead we've been dragging our feet on. Too long, if you ask me."

"Please, Dino," she said through clenched teeth. "Try it—for me?"

"Okay," he sighed, "I'll give it a shot."

"And if that one doesn't fly, then try this one on for size." Here Nina spun her theory about the possibility that competing TV networks just might have taken a hand in the murder.

"No. That's absolutely ridiculous," Rossi scoffed. "Do you really think that multi-billion-dollar corporations would stoop to a thing like murder? What are you snorting these days?"

"I know it sounds farfetched, but you have no idea how cutthroat this business can get. When a studio exec knows he's about to be blown out of the water, there's no telling how far he'll go to beat out the competition. Take one psycho assistant producer whose job is on the line. He's desperate, he'll stop at nothing to—"

"Nina," he broke in, "you can't be serious."

"The man calls on May, makes her an offer he thinks she can't refuse. She refuses. He sweetens the kitty. She still refuses. What's left? To his mind there are worse things than murder. So he digs someone out from under a rock, gives him the address. Whack! No more competition."

"I still don't buy it, dear. You're putting me on, aren't you?"

"I'm *not* putting you on! Will it kill you to have someone do a little more legwork? You'll have to check back on all May's visitors for the past month or so. But isn't it police procedure to check out *all* leads?"

He paused. "I'll have to sleep on that one awhile. It'll be hell to check out. Call you later."

Nina hung up the phone, rechecked her watch. Now it *was* time she got downstairs. Get to Noel before lunch, she decided as she started down the steel steps. See if he knows any retired reporters.

Nina took Sylvia Kastle to The English Garden, one of the noontime haunts she and Dino favored. There, after they both ordered entrees that were only slightly fattening, they caught up on latest developments.

"When will today's tape be aired?" Sylvia asked. She looked smashing in a rust-colored wool suit and a gold-flecked, brown blouse with elegant tan Pancaldi pumps.

"In about three weeks. Lag time is deliberately built in, to provide for emergencies on the set. If one of us got run over by a semi tonight, there'd be time to rewrite."

"They think of everything, don't they?"

Nina dabbed at her mouth with a napkin. "Indeed they do." She regarded Sylvia solicitously. "Things going better today? Butterflies gone?"

"I think I'll make it. Although yesterday, just before the final take, I wished I'd never agreed to do this show."

Nina seized the opening. "And just why *did* you do it?" she asked, for the second time in as many days. "As I understand it, you really don't need the salary, fabulous as it must be."

"You're right, Nina. It was May's doing. 'Get the cobwebs out,' she said. But I think she was more interested in a comeback of her own than in getting rid of mental flab." Her eyes took on a strange, hard light. "Though why she wanted the notoriety, I'll never know."

"How are you getting along with Angela?" Nina asked casually.

Sylvia made a face. "I know now what you meant on Friday. She *is* a bit officious, isn't she? Apparently you two aren't on good terms. She really got upset when I told her we were having lunch. I thought for a minute she might invite herself along." And after a brief pause, "Nina, dear—about May's murder. Have you heard anything further from the police?"

Nina instantly went on guard. Was Sylvia fishing again? Had she picked up any random scuttlebutt from the cast, idle talk about Nina's part in helping solve the Morty Meyer case? About her involvement with Dino Rossi? "Why, no, Sylvia." She fought to keep her face blank. "I haven't heard a thing."

"There was precious little in this morning's paper. Strange how quickly a murder gets forgotten. I just thought . . ." Her voice drifted off. "And our little conversation Friday? You haven't mentioned it to anyone? Those indiscreet things I told you?"

Nina knew it was dangerous, that she might easily blow her cover, but the opportunity to go fishing was irresistible. "Of course not, Sylvia. But it's funny that you should mention it, because I just happened to have a little conversation with Georgine yesterday afternoon, and it was quite an eye-opener."

Sylvia was immediately on guard. "Oh? What did she have to say?"

"Apparently she's somewhat bitter about May. She implied that May was a harder woman to get along with than most people knew. May was quite . . . demanding, according to Georgine, and used to getting her own way."

Sylvia hesitated before answering. "Yes, I guess I'd have to agree. But I prefer to forget such things, now that May's gone. It does no good to dredge up unpleasant memories like that."

Nina took a deep breath and plunged right on. "Another thing she said—and I do hope I'm not telling tales out of school—was that May and Tucker O'Brien had been lovers."

Sylvia sucked in a quick breath, averting her eyes. When she finally spoke, there was a fixed, severe smile on her face. "Georgine has a rather bizarre sense of humor," she said. "I think she was pulling your leg a little, Nina. May and Tucker? Hardly! They lived on entirely different planes. He wasn't her type at all."

She took a careful sip of her tea. "Besides, May would have been eight years older than Tucker. I'm sure that age difference would have been a strong deterrent to . . . romance." She smiled. "No, I wouldn't put any stock in Georgine's little fib. Her story is totally absurd. Actually, it's rather hard to believe that she even told it."

Nina refused to be warned off. Go for broke, she decided. "And what about Georgine herself?" she asked. "Maybe she also had secret designs on Tucker O'Brien? Maybe she's telling all these things by way of smoke-screening certain indiscretions of her own?"

Nina knew immediately she'd gone one step too far. An opaque film glossed over Sylvia's eyes. Her mouth twitched. "Now you *are* stretching things, my dear. Georgine and Tucker? Not in a million years! It's utterly laughable."

Nina forced herself to look at Sylvia head on. They stared eye to eye. It was Sylvia who looked away first, a flustered expression on her face. Nina flashed a conciliatory smile and said, "No harm done? I thought, just so long as we were on the subject . . ."

Sylvia's smile was equally artificial. "Not at all, Nina. It would make an interesting story, wouldn't it? *If* it were true."

Now the woman patted her mouth with her napkin a last time and picked up the check. "I think it's time we were getting back," she said coldly.

There was small talk in the cab as they returned to Meyer Productions, very small indeed, with many long pauses between each exchange.

Now you've done it, Nina thought darkly. Royally blown it. You'll never get another tidbit of information out of Sylvia Kastle.

When Nina got back to her dressing room, she found an urgent message to call Dino. She lost no time getting to the phone.

"Listen, something else has happened, and you're not going to like it." She already knew that from the tone of his voice. "We obtained a copy of May Minton's will from her attorney."

"And? Surprises?"

"A few. She left all her personal possessions to a nephew, Charles Henderson. Lives somewhere on the coast of Maine."

"Somehow I don't think that's the surprise."

"She also left Henderson half a million dollars."

"Is that a motive?"

"It could be when you're about to go bankrupt because your lobster boat has seen better days."

101

"Forget it. A Maine lobster fisherman wouldn't know how to sneak into Carson Place. The smell alone would give him away. There's something else, isn't there?"

"Yeah. She left twenty-five thousand dollars each to Sylvia Kastle and Georgine Dyer, probably for old times' sake. And last, but definitely not least, a neat fifty thousand goes to a buddy of yours—Noel Winston."

Chapter Nine

"Hello? I'd like to speak to Scotty Lane, please."

"You've got him."

"Mr. Lane, you don't know me. A mutual friend gave me your name—"

"Nina McFall, right? What a pleasure."

"Oh, you know me? How—"

"Noel Winston already contacted me, told me you'd be calling. Said I should treat you right, that you're one helluva fine lady."

"Well," Nina said, slightly off balance, "that's what I call service. I only discussed this with Noel yesterday. Did he tell you what I'm looking for?"

"Something about the Glitter Girls, I think."

Nina was nonplussed. "The Glitter Girls?"

"Uh-huh." The voice was gruff and gravelly, yet warm. "That's what we used to call Minton, Kastle and Dyer. They were always into something wild."

"Strange," Nina mused aloud. "The Glitter Girls. And now there's a TV series called *The Golden Girls*. Full circle, it seems."

"Exactly my sentiments. In fact, I'm surprised May and her friends didn't institute a suit when *The Golden Girls* first hit TV. Anyway, they weren't anything like this latest version. When they were in their prime, the Glitter Girls knew how to live it up.'' He chuckled sarcastically. ''With a capital X rating.''

''It certainly sounds like I came to the right man. I asked some of the seniors on the set, but I drew a blank.''

''*Sic transit gloria mundi*,'' Scotty Lane sighed. ''How quickly they forget. Listen, telephone interviews ain't exactly my style, especially when I'm answering the questions. You want to run down here? I'm on West Eleventh, just off Sixth Avenue.''

Nina had a moment's hesitation, but remembered this was a friend of Noel's. Noel with the fifty-thousand-dollar motive. No, Noel her friend with the kind eyes and the darling twin granddaughters. ''Give me the exact address.''

Thirty minutes later, Nina climbed out of a cab and entered a four-story brownstone. Scotty Lane lived on the third floor, rear apartment.

''I could have had the front, but it's quieter in the back,'' he said as they settled in the living room. His place was the classic bachelor apartment, piled everywhere with newspapers, books, and magazines, the furniture shabby but comfortable, and the room smelling faintly of cigarette smoke and bourbon. Nina felt as though she'd settled down in a pleasant bar somewhere.

She studied Scotty Lane for a moment. Impressions based on telephone conversations are rarely accurate, and this was no exception. Instead of the William Conrad clone she'd expected, Scotty was extremely short and extremely thin. He was also extremely bald and extremely likeable. They automatically went onto a first-name basis.

''I want to tell you, Nina, how much I enjoy you on the show. Never was a great one for soaps, but since I quit the paper I find myself vegetating a little. I started watching *The Turning Seasons* and got hooked. Kingston Falls reminds me of the town I grew up in. And Melanie Prescott reminds me of a lot of obnoxious ladies I've tangled with in my lifetime.''

"Thanks for the kind words. I . . . we try to please.''

"No snow job, Nina. You do good work. You bring a lot of authority to the role. This *Golden Girls* rip-off idea sounds good. Noel told me about it. He and I go way back. Great guy. I'll be looking forward to it. I'm only sorry that May got nicked. She'd have been a gas. She was one smart cookie. Nobody ever pushed her around.''

"Sounds like you really knew them. Did you do celebrity features?''

"It wasn't my usual beat, only now and then, when somebody got sick. I was on the city desk mostly, prowling the back alleys at City Hall, if you know what I mean. But once I started covering the Glitter Girls I always kept my eyes on those birds. So, what can I do for you?''

"Did Noel tell you I was the one who discovered May . . . the day she was murdered?''

"Check. That must have been a real kick in the gut.''

"It was. May was special to me, and though I know it's none of my affair, I can't help but be curious about what happened. I've been talking to Sylvia and Georgine, and I keep getting all sorts of conflicting reports. I'd like to talk to someone who knew them in their prime, who knew what they were really like in the early days, particularly May. Before we met, I had an impression of a sort of cross between a grand duchess and a saint. But then she told me the most outrageous thing about herself.''

"May never knew when to keep her mouth shut.''

Nina giggled. "The very first day I met her, she casually mentioned that she used a telescope to watch people across the way. A *telescope*!"

Scotty snorted his amusement. "There's a story behind that. The telescope was an opening-night gag gift a long time ago. Actors used to give each other dopey little presents on opening night—maybe they still do. To kind of help take away the first-night jitters, I guess. Anyway, on the opening night of some potboiler they were both in, Sylvia gave May this telescope. I don't know why, maybe the play had a nautical theme or something. The story goes that everyone expected this bomb was gonna open and close on the same night, a real stinker. So May figured, what the hell, might as well have some fun with it, and she took this telescope on stage with her and started to clown around."

"That's very unprofessional, but it sounds just like her. Was she fired?"

"Damn near. The director was gonna dump her until he read the reviews the next morning. Sonofabitch if she wasn't the hit of the evening. The critics all singled her out and gave her the biggest set of raves she ever had. From then on she could write her own ticket. She figured the telescope was her good-luck piece, and every play or movie she was in, she got that damn telescope in somehow. She'd have it on a table nearby, or she'd pick it up for a second and then put it right down. I remember once she threw it at a dog that was digging up her garden—in this movie, I mean."

Nina studied his face carefully. "Are you making this up?"

"Would I lie to you? When she pitched the thing at the dog, her aim was so good she broke the poor mutt's leg. Naturally in Hollywood a dog ain't just a dog, especially not when you break its leg, and the owner brought suit for a ton of money. You know, special dog, special training, loss of income, trauma for the pup, all that stuff. May paid every penny. The press had a field day with that one. Put her right on page one.''

''Are you implying that if Sylvia hadn't given May that dumb little gift, May might never have become a star?''

''Not at all. But I think May probably felt that way. Anyway, when Sylvia announced her retirement, May decided to make the grand gesture and give it back to her.''

''But May still has it. I saw it.''

''That's right. After May told Sylvia she was going to give her the lucky prop, she decided she couldn't part with it after all. So she sneaked out and had a copy made and gave Sylvia the fake. Sylvia didn't care, so everybody was happy.''

Obviously Nina had come to the right place. Scotty Lane seemed to be the world's foremost authority on the Glitter Girls and could probably keep her entertained with anecdotes for hours.

''Scotty, tell me about May's involvement with the Tucker O'Brien murder. Something about that story doesn't ring right.''

Scotty Lane laughed. ''That's the understatement of the year. Tell me what you need, Nina.''

''Let's be blunt. What about . . . ah . . . May Minton's sex life?''

''May went through men like some gals go through Kleenex. I came in sideways on her once, asked her how come. She gave me some half-assed reply about an ugly childhood.''

''But when Tucker O'Brien came along?''

''Complete turnaround. It was like someone took her into the woodshed and gave her a good blister-

107

ing. She was a good girl ever after. Crazy about that no-good bastard.''

"So those stories about him were true? Sylvia says she was in love with him. Maybe she would have married him.''

"Ah, Sylvia embroiders for effect. She always did that. If it was female, soft, warm, and smelled nice, Tucker was hot to trot.''

"Now I'm wondering about Georgine as well.''

"Wonder no more. He had 'em all. Not all at once, of course. He started out with Georgine.''

Nina was incredulous. "But she's such a mousey type.''

"Not in those days. She was the prettiest of the three of them, and she was crazy about Tucker. The affair lasted a couple of months, which, for old Tucker, might have been a record. Then he probably just got tired of Georgine and dumped her for Sylvia.''

"How could Georgine ever work with Sylvia after that?''

"Oh, when Tucker dumped them, he did it with style and a lot of soothing little souvenirs, like jewelry and furs and cars. Anyway, Georgine was so naive, I'll bet she didn't even know about Sylvia until after Tucker dumped Sylvia and went on to May.''

"How did Sylvia take it?''

"Right in stride. She was no dope about the guys. And the thing with May didn't last very long, either.''

"Sounds like half the women in Hollywood had a motive for murdering Tucker O'Brien.''

"Half the women and their husbands. So nobody was too surprised or too sad when the cops found Tucker dead in that infamous bedroom of his, a bullet hole in his head.''

108

"Do you think one of the Glitter Girls did it?"

"Nobody was ever able to prove anything. Oh, all kinds of crazy rumors went around. But they never found the murder weapon; they never found the murderer." He laughed bitterly. "One of the classic, unsolved murder mysteries of the decade."

"But you think it might have been May who killed O'Brien? Or Sylvia or Georgine?"

"I didn't say that. You gotta draw your own conclusions. But I bet that if we ever got some sodium pentathol into one of those ladies, we'd get the truth. They know. May knew. Only she isn't talking anymore."

"But how, with leads like that, could the police not get a conviction?"

Lane's chuckle was sly. "Maybe they weren't really trying all that hard."

"Pressure was brought to bear? A lot of money changed hands?"

"What else? May and her pals were on the top of the heap in those days. They were under contract for two TV specials a year. They were starring in an SRO Broadway show. It was to somebody's advantage to see that their headliners' names didn't get dragged in the mud."

"How soon after the O'Brien killing did May retire?"

"Too soon, if you ask me. She didn't have to retire, but it seemed to take the steam out of her. Not only did she retire, but she went into hiding. Sylvia bowed out a few months later and then she got married and started acting like Lady Astor. Georgine put away her makeup case just about the same time, but she didn't get married until only a few years ago. Meanwhile she made a nice name for herself as a film historian. You know, saving old movies from crumbling away in the vaults, that kind of stuff.

They gave her a special nod at the Oscar show a few years back, but she didn't show up for it.''

Scotty paused and cleared his throat. "Listen, Nina, I'm only too happy to be of help. In fact, I'm honored. But tell me, just what exactly is it you're trying to dig out here?"

Nina leaned forward earnestly. "Why was May Minton killed?"

"That I'm afraid I can't help you with, Nina. Only May Minton—and her murderer—could answer that one."

"Do you think Sylvia Kastle and Georgine Dyer know?" Nina persisted. "They must. Otherwise, why this cat-and-mouse game they're playing with me? Sylvia even visited me at my apartment and pumped me for details about the murder scene the day after it happened. She wanted to know what the cops said, whether there were any suspects . . ."

"Not too subtle, is she?" Scotty said with a wry grin.

"Tell me, Scotty, who'd have the kind of money it would take to shut down the Tucker O'Brien investigation? And how would they go about it?"

He had a coughing fit again. "Hell, one of the gals could have dug up enough scratch to buy off the crucial people. It wasn't the first time; it won't be the last. Nasty old world we live in, darling."

"What about the men they married? Sylvia tells me her husband is a big-time real estate developer. Georgine's husband is connected with City Hall in some way. Could they have been involved?"

"You're forgetting one thing, Nina. They didn't come onto the scene and marry Sylvia and Georgine until long after all this happened. It was ancient history by then."

Nina sighed. "Yes, that's right."

"They're powerhouses, all right. Don't doubt it

for a minute. Lance Kirby has connections up the kazoo. Up *and* down. From City Hall to the mobbies. Old Carbon Six.''

''Carbon Six?'' Nina echoed, puzzled.

''That was a nickname we had for him. He was Lanislau Kirbonsyzk then. He's Polish or Latvian, something like that. Pronounced kirbon-*sick*. He changed it to Kirby after he got married. Sylvia's doing, I expect.''

''How do you spell it?''

''Good question. I used to be proud of the fact that I could do it without a check. K-I-R-B-O-N-S-Y-Z-K. I think that's right.''

''Interesting. And Georgine's husband?''

''Earnest Claypool's a power-broker type, too. He knows where all the skeletons are hidden down at City Hall. I wouldn't suggest you go bucking him, either. That is, if you're thinking of pursuing this thing further. Are you?''

''I can't really say. I think I'll keep snooping around. Maybe something will turn up.''

''Like a shroud. Whoever wanted Minton out of the way certainly wouldn't quibble about giving you an early grave, too. Take my advice, Nina. Let it go. You're outta your depth here.''

''I suppose you're right, Scotty. But . . .''

''Tell you what,'' he said. ''I'll go down to the paper later on today, talk to some of my old buddies there. I'll go through the morgue and pull the Glitter Girls files, see if anything jumps out at me. I have some old police contacts, too. It won't hurt to ask a few questions, see if I can get any additional angle on how come May got on somebody's hit list at this late date. Where can I reach you?''

Nina gave him her studio and home number and her Primrose Towers address as well. ''If I find anything,'' he grunted, ''I'll make some photocopies,

111

put 'em in an envelope, bring 'em over. It'd give me an excuse to see you again. Maybe you'd even give me an autograph or something. For my daughter-in-law, of course." He laughed. "People always say that, don't they?"

"Really, Scotty, you shouldn't put yourself out on my account. You've already done enough. I'd be happy to send you all the autographed photos you can use without that."

"Nonsense. I've got nothing else to do with my time." He chuckled hoarsely. "Except watch the soaps. Hell, this thing's got me curious now. I liked that old broad. She had her faults, but she was people, too. That was a helluva dirty way to die."

"Well, whatever you can do. And if I'm out, you can always leave the package with the security guard. Either way, call me and let me know how things are going. I truly appreciate your interest, Scotty."

"Forget about it. The old blood's pumping—I feel alive for the first time in months. Maybe this one will go front page, who knows?"

For a long time after she returned from seeing Scotty Lane, Nina sat in a corner of her kitchen, staring into space. What a sweetheart, she conceded, amazed at the quick rapport that had built between them. She felt as if she'd known Scotty all her life.

Her thoughts drifted to knottier points of the just-concluded conversation. Where would she go from here? Whom should she approach for information now? What was the keystone? Had something happened in May Minton's life recently to tip the scales so drastically, to trigger her murder? Surely there must be someone besides Sylvia and Georgine who had some inkling of the decision that had nudged

May's murderer off dead center. And since she couldn't expect to get a straight answer from the remaining Glitter Girls . . .

Thoughts of Horst Krueger and Helen Meyer surfaced. A gut flash, nothing more. They were, after all, the ones who'd coaxed May out of retirement. Maybe May had revealed something that would give her a clue to the killer's motive.

Ridiculous. And yet, what other option did she have? It was very likely that May might have revealed some vital clue during those prolonged conversations. May was a notorious babbler. Certainly Helen wouldn't recognize a clue if she tripped over it. But if Rossi were turned loose on her . . . Of course! Dino had every reason to call on Helen Meyer and Horst Krueger, to pose hypothetical questions concerning the murder. He would balk, of course, hung up as he was on the Angela Dolan angle. Just look at how stubborn he'd been when she'd suggested he dig out the file on Tucker O'Brien.

Thoughts of Rossi reminded her that they had a date for 7:30 this evening. They were taking Peter to a pizza place for supper—another togetherness strategem which Nina herself had suggested, a way of including the boy in their flowering relationship. So what if Peter had chosen a place called Val's Pizza Corral? How bad could it be?

Chapter Ten

Val's Pizza Corral was about what Nina had envisioned—tacky city. Western motifs prevailed, with mountains, deserts, cacti and sagebrush painted on the walls and fake, weathered-wood fencing skirting the whole of the drafty, barny room. The place crawled with kids. Cowboy clowns roamed from table to table, passing out balloons to the toddlers while an automated hillbilly band played on a stage at the far end. One could hardly hear over the din.

Oh, well, Nina thought, regarding the eager-eyed, dark-haired boy as he ordered the house special, aptly named Dead Man's Gullet. Join the fun. She ordered the same.

Equally attractive was the adjoining room that sported video games, bucking broncos, bowling, darts—you name it, they had it—that Peter already had in his sights.

"Having fun?" Dino asked the twelve-year-old boy as the Dead Man's Gullet was smacked down in front of him.

"Sure, Dad," he said enthusiastically, his eyes aglow. "This is great. What a cool place!"

"And the pizza? Okay?"

"Great, Dad. They make wonderful pizzas here."

He frowned. "How about yours? Is yours okay, Nina?"

Nina mugged outrageously, laughing. "Listen, this is *memorable*."

"Good," he said, "I'm glad you dig it. We'll have to come here again real soon."

Dino winked at her, and she rolled her eyes as she guided a long, stringy strand of cheese into her mouth.

Despite the bluegrass blare and the babble of kiddy voices, Nina was actually having fun. There was a good feeling about being together with Dino and his son, about sharing this warm experience. Family. She smiled. Even though she wasn't at all sure that she was ready for a family as yet. Not a secondhand one, at any rate.

Looking at Dino, handsome in a light blue sportshirt and blue blazer and at Peter in jeans and a sweatshirt, she felt her heart fill up. Good for a woman's morale, she conceded. Peter was a beautiful boy, and bore a striking resemblance to his father. That mane of glossy black hair, the tawny olive complexion, those huge brown eyes that seemed to explore her soul, and the sensitive mouth, all were just like his dad's. He was a honey all right, his lapses into brattiness notwithstanding. She handled his rebelliousness better than Dino most of the time.

"I can't eat any more," Peter announced abruptly, his pizza only half gone. "Can we take the rest home? I can microwave it for breakfast tomorrow."

Rossi's smile was indulgent. "Yes, son, I think that can be arranged."

Nina couldn't resist. "Pizza for breakfast? Sounds yummy. Sure you don't want some sauerkraut and ice cream with it?"

Peter sent her a wise-guy grin. "Don't knock it if

you haven't tried it. Hey, Dad, can I go play some games now? Can I have some quarters? You wanna come along?''

"No, not right now. Nina and I want to talk a little bit. Maybe we'll join you later."

"Sure," Peter said, "just so long's all you do is talk."

"Okay, Monstro," Nina scolded playfully. "Enough. Here . . ." she reached for her bag, "I've got some quarters."

"I've got it," Dino said sternly, a slight edge to his voice.

"Oops." Nina put on a contrite look. "I forgot I'm back in macho land."

Rossi glowered. "What's that supposed to mean?" Peter asked.

"Never mind." Rossi pressed three dollar bills into his hand. "Go get change. Play your games."

"So?" he said when Peter hurried off. "How is it so far? Enjoying yourself?"

"How can you ask? To think I've been missing this all my life."

"Peter's having a great time. That's what's important, isn't it?"

Nina reached across the table, put her hand over his. "Yes. And I *am* having fun. Just being pesky. Peter seems so much more lively tonight, more sure of himself."

"You can take credit for that. He never stops talking about you. You've really made a hit with the guy. And you do look especially lovely tonight. Your hair, your eyes . . . You drive me crazy, you know that?"

Nina switched the subject, in a deliberate attempt to damp the afterburners. "How was your day? Any luck?"

"I've got some good news and some bad news."

116

"Give me the good news first."

"Your theory about possible network complicity."

Nina's heart leaped. "Yes?"

He shook his head. "I don't know how you do it, but you were right again. On the button. We finished running down the last of the people on Miss Minton's visitors' register just this afternoon. And big as life, a guy named Vance Dunnigan. Director of properties and acquisitions for your network's arch rival. He called on May two weeks ago."

"Dino," Nina said excitedly, "how wonderful! What did this Mr. Dunnigan have to say for himself?"

"Not so fast. We haven't contacted him yet. We only broke it this afternoon, remember? Tomorrow Charley and I'll pay him a visit and ask some hard questions."

Nina beamed. "And what about Angela?"

"She's on hold. I'm deferring to that crazy intuition of yours. After we question this Dunnigan guy, if it doesn't pay off, we're moving in."

Nina frowned. "Dino, I hate to be a nag, but I still say you're way off base on that one." She sipped her coffee. "And now the bad news?"

"Those police files on the Tucker O'Brien murder?"

"What about them?"

"I found the warehouse and got permission to crack the files. The man led me to the proper pile of boxes. We went through them with a fine-toothed comb. Might as well have stayed home. They're gone. Every damned file."

"Are you sure?" Nina asked, astonished. "There's no chance that you were looking in the wrong place?"

"Nope. We came up with one folder with the ID

number, O'Brien's name, and the date on it. Empty, of course. We were in the right box, all right. Someone just beat us to it."

"That *is* a kick in the teeth." She paused, reflecting. "It's a clear indication that we're on the right track, wouldn't you say? May's murder *is* connected to Tucker O'Brien's somehow."

"Maybe yes, maybe no. Those files could have been stolen sixteen years ago. If your theory about his murder being 'fixed' back in nineteen seventy-two holds any water, that is. Whoever got paid off could have seen to it then."

"Or someone influential could have done it in the last week or so. There could have been something in those files that would hang May's murderer. And aren't the husbands, Lance Kirby and Earnest Claypool, heavy enough in city politics to engineer a thing like that?"

"Lance Kirby and Earnest Claypool? Now where did you come up with those guys? Who told you about them?"

Nina sent him a wise-owl smile. "I knew. Then I was talking to a man today, an old-time reporter, who gave me some extra insights into the picture."

Rossi released a long-suffering sigh. "Okay, Nina. Level with me. What have you been up to now?"

Briefly she related her conversation with Scotty Lane. In particular, she emphasized again the fact that May Minton's life had never been in jeopardy until she agreed to sign on with TTS.

"Hey," Rossi said, "are you intimating that Sylvia and Georgine know what the missing piece to the puzzle is? *And* that, just possibly, someone else on the TTS set also knew that something new was coming down, something big enough to nudge someone into murder? But what could it be?"

"I have no idea. Not at this point, anyway. Maybe

tomorrow something will come to me. But for now, our only remaining option . . ."

Rossi finished the thought for her. ". . . is to question Helen Meyer and Horst Krueger, who talked Minton into coming onto the show in the first place. I'll get on it the first thing tomorrow, after I run down that network barracuda."

Nina suddenly decided to take a gamble. "Dino, listen. Just now you said something nice about my hunches paying off on the network lead."

"So?" She knew the look; he was on guard already. But she went ahead anyhow.

"I've got another one."

"Nina . . ."

"Let me finish, please. I keep thinking that we're missing something obvious, and the best place to look would be back in May's apartment."

"Come on, Nina. It's been combed thoroughly."

"I know it has, but not—" she stopped herself, but too late.

"Not by you? Is that what you were going to say?"

"No. Not by *us*."

He grinned. "Nice save. Okay, not by us. What do you think we'd find?"

"I don't know. I don't even know if there's anything to be found. But I think we might learn something. Please? Isn't it worth a try?"

"Could be. When do you want to go?"

"Now. Tonight. Let's take Peter home so Mrs. Bartolucci can tuck him in, and then scoot right over to Carson Place."

"Not exactly the evening I had in mind."

"Oh, not for long. Just a look around. Just ten minutes, to satisfy my itch."

But as it turned out, they were at the Minton apartment a lot longer than ten minutes.

"Let's make it fast," Dino muttered as soon as they were inside. There was an eerie silence in the apartment that Nina didn't like.

"This place is too well built. You can't even hear street noises," she said, going to the window.

"Baby, the clock is ticking. You don't want to waste your ten minutes looking at the view."

"I was just remembering something May told me the first day I came here. She used to spy on the people in the next building for kicks."

"She must have had terrific eyesight."

"No, she used a telescope."

"What?"

"She used a telescope. . . . What's the matter?"

"There was no telescope in this place," Dino said slowly and distinctly. "Why didn't you tell me?"

"Is it important?"

"Nina, come on! She was bludgeoned and no weapon was found."

Nina gasped. "Oh God, you mean she might have been killed with her lucky prop? That's too much!"

"At least now we know what we're looking for," Dino said.

They wandered through the apartment, reviewing all the facts, thrashing out every theory either of them could think of, but nothing further emerged. In the bedroom, Nina's eye fell on the television set. "That's probably as good as the day it was bought," she said. "May told me she only watched news programs and quiz shows. And *The Turning Seasons*, of course. I wonder. She was probably just flattering me."

"Doesn't make sense," Rossi muttered, shaking his head.

120

"What doesn't?"

"An old woman who used to be a hell-raiser lives like a recluse, rarely goes out, and doesn't even watch TV much. Maybe she rented video tapes and ran old movies on the VCR?"

"I doubt it. She said she couldn't stand to see herself the way she used to be."

"Let's just test that statement. She left a tape in it."

Dino pushed a few buttons and the waiting machinery popped into action. The VCR gears began to hum and Nina was astonished to see May's image on the screen. There was no sound track whatsoever.

"Never believe anything an actor tells you," Dino said with a maddening smirk. "Probably spent all day watching her old flicks."

"No—look, it's changed to something else. That was just a short clip from some old movie. This is a clip from a different one. Start it again—rewind it and start it again." Nina sat down in front of the screen, thoroughly absorbed.

The tape ran for less than five minutes. It consisted of a series of short clips, all from May Minton's films, with no seeming connection or continuity.

"I don't get it," Dino said.

"Neither do I," Nina replied. "But I'm going to. Run it again."

They watched the short cassette three more times, but nothing new surfaced to explain the mystifying clips. Dino suggested they leave, and Nina wordlessly moved to the door, deep in thought.

"You'd think," he said, "that if she wanted to look at herself she'd have prints of all her movies. What's with these short clips?"

"I don't know. I can't understand what she was

. . . Dino, I've got it! I bet they're outtakes—scenes that never made it into the final films!''

Nina raced back into the bedroom and started the VCR again. She fairly bounced up and down on May's bed in excitement.

"Look! Look at what she's doing."

On the screen, May was standing by a fireplace, talking to someone unseen.

"She's standing and talking."

"Right, but there's more. Look at the mantelpiece. What's on it?"

"A pair of candle holders, a vase of flowers, two books, a telescope—holy shit, is that it? The telescope?"

"It's got to be. Now watch the next one."

After that, the game of find-the-telescope was easy. In clip after clip, the ornate brass instrument showed up, sometimes in the background, sometimes in May's hand.

The last clip was the strangest outtake of all. It was an exterior shot in which May was holding the telescope absentmindedly as Sylvia passed in front of her. May, all innocence, suddenly landed the instrument on Sylvia's head, producing a raging reaction that couldn't possibly have been rehearsed. Instantly, Sylvia snatched the telescope away and threw herself on May with arms flailing as an assortment of people rushed in from the sidelines to separate the two women.

Nina repeated to Dino everything Scotty Lane had told her about the telescope. As she talked, each detail of the seemingly meaningless anecdote took on fresh possible significance.

"Now we not only have a pretty good idea what the murder weapon was, but we know something else," Nina said as they left May's apartment.

"Yeah. We know somebody is trying to tell us something. But what and who?"

"One thing at a time."

When Dino pulled up to Primrose Towers, Nina resisted the urge to invite him up for a nightcap. "I have some pretty big scenes to go over for tomorrow morning, and somehow I don't think I'd get much studying done with you around," she murmured, extricating herself from a particularly long and ardent kiss. "Good night, darling. I'll call you tomorrow as soon as I get a break. Meanwhile, let's both think about that video tape."

Dino had it on the seat beside him; it would be heading for the lab first thing in the morning. Perhaps the cassette hadn't yet yielded all its secrets.

As Nina entered the lobby of her building, Willie, the night security guard, hailed her. "Got something here for you, Ms. McFall," he said. "Came in an hour or so ago."

A package? She wasn't expecting anything. But when she saw the manila envelope, she remembered her conversation with Scotty this morning. He must have found something and dropped it off while she was out. Nina tucked the envelope under her arm and rode the elevator to the thirty-sixth floor.

Once inside, she took off her jacket and kicked off her shoes. Though she knew she should leave Scotty's research until morning—she did have lines to learn—she was curious, and, taking a letter opener from her desk, ripped open the envelope.

Nina's blood turned cold as she looked at the hideously mutilated face staring at her from a glossy eight-by-ten photograph. She instantly identified the woman as a model whose once-beautiful face had been slashed by her razor-wielding former lover.

123

This very photo had been on the front pages of all the tabloids. Where on earth had it come from? Certainly not from Scotty.

Gingerly, Nina turned the photo over, looking for some identifying mark. What she found instead was a message made up of words cut from magazines and newspapers:

"YOU WANT TO LOOK LIKE THIS, NINA? LAY OFF, OR ELSE!"

Nina thought for a minute she was going to be sick. Terror sent a paralyzing shudder the length of her body. Trembling, she went to the phone and punched out Dino's home number. It seemed like hours until he answered.

"Dino," she said, fighting to keep her voice steady, "something's happened. Could you come over right away?"

Chapter Eleven

When Rossi arrived, within half an hour of Nina's call, she was relatively composed. Even so, she flung herself into his arms and clung to him for a few moments.

As Nina gradually calmed down, they reviewed the day's events, but there had been nothing to shed light on the source of the photograph. Dino examined the picture thoroughly, both front and back.

"This could have come from some ambulance-chasing news photographer, or it could have been lifted from police files. But there should be a mark of some sort on the back. Photographers are fanatical about their credit lines. I'll see if anyone downtown recognizes this shot, but it's doubtful."

He picked up the envelope. It was brand-new and bore only Nina's name and address, including her apartment number, all neatly printed. "How many people have your home address?"

"I don't give it out as a rule, but a lot of people have access to it through the TTS directory."

"How many?"

"Everyone connected to the show."

"Does the directory include your apartment number?"

"No, it doesn't!" Her elation quickly dissolved.

"But I've had a lot of those people here, at parties. Oh, Dino, this isn't getting us anywhere."

"You're right. Still, I want you to make a list of every cast and crew member who's ever been to this apartment."

She looked at him incredulously. "There are dozens! Are you going to check out every one of them?

He grinned at her. "Of course not. I'll have somebody else do it. And you better watch it; your disdain for standard procedure is showing."

The zinger got to her. "I don't disdain your routines. It's just that they take so long."

"Whereas you need only a split second to take your psychic temperature and come up with a winner."

"Psychic temperature! You really don't have much of an opinion of my results, do you? Maybe you'd like it better if I—"

He took her by both shoulders in a sudden embrace that surprised both of them.

"I'd like it better if things like this didn't happen to you. I worry about you," he said with harsh intensity. Then his voice dropped to the deep-throated pitch that always sent shivers up and down her legs. "I need you. Don't you understand? I love having you in my work, but I need you in my life."

It was a moment that Nina would willingly have prolonged indefinitely.

"Yes, I do understand. And I love you for worrying about me."

"Nina, how obvious have you been in your snooping around?"

She admitted that she hadn't been overly careful while talking to people right after May Minton was killed. Anyone on the set could have figured out that Nina was more than a little interested in the murder. "But everyone's interested. The only slightly unusual thing I've done is to get Scotty Lane's name and number. But I can't remember anyone within earshot when that happened."

"There was one person."

"Dino! You can check Noel Winston out until you collect retirement pay, but I'm here to tell you you'll be wasting your time."

"That's exactly why I want you to drop this case."

"What!"

"Your intuition is almost as strong as your stubbornness. You're probably right about Winston, but we don't really *know* that. Don't you see? You're willing to take risks based on intuition, but I'm not willing for you to take any risks at all."

"I *don't* take—"

"Listen to me. Somebody is paying a lot of attention to what you do and what you say. And you may be a brilliant intuitive sleuth, my love," he paused to let the compliment sink in, "but you're a disaster at covering your trail. I can't risk your safety. I love you too much."

The fervent declaration tempted her to agree, to stay wrapped in his protective embrace forever. But she knew herself too well.

"No way, love," she said firmly. "You can't get rid of me that easily. You can tell me to get off the case till doomsday, but that doesn't mean I'm going to do it. I'm involved in this thing even more deeply than you are—remember, I'm the one who found May's body! I can't wipe that out of my mind just because some nut sends me a poison-pen letter."

Dino sighed in frustration. "What am I going to do with a stubborn mule like you?"

Nina smiled impishly. "I can think of a few things. Too bad we don't have time to explore the possibilities."

"Want me to stay the night?" Dino asked, pulling her into his arms.

"Yes, but you better not. I really have to get at to-morrow's script—I'm way behind."

They settled for a series of long, devouring kisses at the door. Dino, Dino, she thought after locking herself in. What's going to happen to us?

In her dressing room the following morning, Nina stared at her reflection in the mirror. Momentarily the lovely face before her became distorted and bloody, criss-crossed by gaping slash marks. She recoiled from the image and shuddered. A week ago today, she reminisced, her stomach tightening, I went to May Minton's apartment and discovered her, dead in her bathtub. Only a week? It seemed a month had passed since she'd stumbled upon the grisly scene.

She shook her head, fought to concentrate. *Come on!* she scolded. You've got a blocking rehearsal in half an hour, and you hardly know any of your lines.

And what was next? Last night's surge of confidence was fading fast. She recalled the warning she'd received at this selfsame dressing table in the Morty Meyer fiasco. She also recalled the way that warning was reinforced—by forty pounds of steel that crashed onto the set, barely missing her head. That's what came of disregarding warnings. Would she be so lucky this time?

With that she gathered her script and locked her dressing room door, fighting to shake off a cold chill, an all pervading sense of doom. Then she started down to the soundstage.

The mood this morning was quite different, and Nina couldn't get over a sense of disorientation, the feeling of being a stranger on her own turf as she came into the main studio.

The reason for the different mood was immediately apparent. Occasionally the TTS writers felt it was important to reinforce Melanie Prescott's executive powers by taking the action out of her private office and into the corporate halls, which meant hiring additional actors. Horst and Helen usually fought the additional costs involved, but every few weeks they lost the battle and hired a group of extras to portray corporate executives, secretaries, messengers, and assorted help. Apparently this was one of those days, yet the extras seemed to be the only people not avoiding Nina as she crossed the hall.

Ridiculous, Nina reassured herself. You're letting your imagination get the best of you. But wasn't everyone being cool?

Her start-the-day-with-a-smile sword-cross with Angela Dolan went largely ignored. "Oh, it's you, Nina," she remarked absently. "So nice of you to make it," Angela muttered as quickly she turned away, returning to her coffee and Danish.

Now, working her way through the obstacle course of tangled power cords and camera cables as she approached the set representing Melanie Prescott's office, Nina overtook Georgine Dyer. "Here, Georgine," she said, taking her left elbow in effort to stabilize her, "let me help you." She smiled down at the older woman. "How've you been? Are you getting a handle on our routine here?"

Georgine's face was a mask. "I'm fine, thank you. There's no need for any of that. I'm not quite ready for a nursing home yet, appearances to the contrary."

Nina kept her aplomb. "No offense intended, Georgine," she said brightly. "Just thought I'd play Girl Scout for a change."

"I don't need any help." Georgine's glare would have made ice cubes. "Now if you'll excuse me . . ." With that she turned away.

After the blocking session was over, Nina decided to test the waters with Sylvia Kastle. Approaching her at the coffee maker, she mustered up a radiant smile. "Good morning, Sylvia. How are you today?"

"Fine, thanks." Her gaze remained veiled, no trace of a smile crossing her face.

"I'm hearing wonderful things about you and Georgine," Nina continued, forcing gaiety. "Didn't I say that you and Georgine had absolutely nothing to worry about? I understand you two just had the cast in stitches yesterday."

A faint trace of a smile threatened to emerge, but didn't. "Thank you for the kind words." Sylvia turned to walk away, but Nina deliberately shifted, blocking her escape.

"How about having lunch again, Sylvia?" Twist the dagger, she told herself, *make* her react. "My treat this time. Tomorrow, perhaps?"

"I'm afraid not. I'm booked."

"But . . ." Nina was left talking to herself, as Sylvia stalked away.

"Well," the jovial male voice boomed behind her, "that was about as good an example of the cold shoulder as I've ever seen."

She turned to find Noel Winston beaming at her. "Noel," she quipped. "You're actually *talking* to me! I'd begun to think my deodorant had failed or something."

"What do you mean?" Winston said, a benign, admiring light in his eyes. "I'd talk to *you* anytime, anywhere. Fight dragons for the chance."

"Aren't you sweet? Thanks, I needed that."

Nina took the opportunity to study Noel Winston's face. Was there anything different about him? Did he look guilty? Worried? Was this the face of a man who's just learned he's inherited a small fortune? None of the above. Maybe May Minton's attorney hadn't contacted Noel yet. How long did those things take? Never having been mentioned in anyone's will, Nina had no idea.

"Did you get in touch with my friend Scotty Lane yet?" Noel asked now.

"Scotty's a regular sweetheart, just like you. We had a most interesting chat. In fact, he's even doing some legwork for me, chasing down some information I asked about."

"You certainly know how to twist us old geezers around your little finger, don't you?" Noel said affectionately.

Nina smiled. "I don't intentionally set out to do that, Noel. It's just that you're all so easy."

He laughed heartily. "Easy come, easy go. What's this guff about nobody talking to you? You're the sweetheart of the regiment, and you know it."

Nina raised one brow. "Tell that to Angela. And to Georgine, and, of course, Sylvia. They act like I'm Typhoid Mary."

"Don't worry about it, honey," Noel soothed. "Everybody's a little on edge today, what with all these new faces on the scene. It'll all come out in the wash, believe me."

This dear man a cold-blooded murderer? Impossible! Nina said to herself as she kissed him gently on the cheek. "Thanks again for putting me in touch with Scotty," she said. "I like him very much."

Noel gave her a broad wink. "And I'm sure he likes *you* very much. Scotty's a sucker for a pretty face. See you later, Nina—have to go run lines with Robin."

Mention of Scotty Lane reminded Nina that she'd promised to autograph some glossies for him. She decided to stop by Publicity and pick up a batch of photos before lunch—her supply was running low. As she started out of the studio, she heard her name being called over the public address system, "Nina McFall,

131

Nina McFall—telephone call in the front office. Nina McFall—telephone.''

Nina winced, glad that none of the "powers that be" were anywhere in sight. Cast and crew members were strongly discouraged from receiving personal calls during rehearsals, except in the case of dire emergency. Her heartbeat speeded up in sudden apprehension. The first thing that came to mind was that something had happened to Dino. She dashed to the front office and picked up the phone with a trembling hand. Her worst fears were immediately confirmed when she heard a brisk voice say, "Ms. McFall, this is Midtown General Hospital . . .''

"Oh, my God!" Nina gasped. "It's Dino Rossi, isn't it?" Visions of Dino's strong, muscular body covered with blood, lying on a gurney, filled her mind. A police detective's life was constantly in danger. Had he been shot, stabbed, beaten?

"This is *Midtown General Hospital,*" the voice repeated very slowly and loudly. "A hit-and-run victim was admitted to Emergency last night. When he regained consciousness, he asked that we contact you.''

"*What's his name*?" Nina practically screamed into the receiver.

"Scott Alexander Lane," said the voice.

It took a moment for the name to register. When it did, Nina's eyes widened in shock. "Scotty Lane? Dear Lord!''

Chapter Twelve

For long moments after the nurse admitted Nina into Scotty Lane's room, neither of them spoke. The institutional clock on the wall read 5:41; it had taken the cab more than an hour to thread its way through the late afternoon traffic. Nina stood motionless at the foot of Scotty's bed, not sure he was conscious.

The nurse finished winding up his bed slightly, plumped his pillows, and left them alone. Slowly Scotty opened his eyes.

"Did you bring those pictures?" he said, spacing the words carefully, the effort to talk plainly taking its toll.

"Pictures?" Nina said, moving to his side. The only picture that came to mind was that of the mutilated model. Goose bumps scudded along her arms. How could Scotty Lane possibly know about that?

"Yeah, you were gonna autograph some photos of yourself for me, remember?"

"Oh," she breathed. "*Those* pictures. I was thinking of something else. No, I didn't. I came here straight from the studio. Publicity shots were the last thing on my mind. I've been so worried!"

Awkward silence closed in again as she looked down at Scotty, trying to get a fix on his physical features through all the bandages and the myriad tubes that obscured his face.

"Scotty," she said finally, "what happened? The doctor said you were hit by a car. An accident. Is that how it happened?"

"Right. Only it wasn't any accident, not by a long shot. That guy was laying for me. He wanted to kill me."

Nina gasped. This was worse than she'd thought. Somehow, someone had tracked down Scotty Lane, knowing that he was helping her. So it was all her fault.

"Tell me the whole thing, Scotty," she said. "Start at the very beginning. From the time I left you yesterday until now."

The story, told in fits and starts, between many painful pauses and gaspings for breath, was simple. Scotty had intended to leave his apartment right after they talked. But inertia being what it was at his age, he hadn't started out until a few hours later. He took the bus to his old newspaper building and spent almost two hours scouring records, culling clips from the Glitter Girls files, photocopying those he thought shed the strongest light on their lifestyles, marking pertinent sections.

It was almost four by then, and he proceeded to the Midtown North precinct, where he still knew a few old-timers on the squad there. Lieutenant Torgeson, a rookie cop when they'd first met, was extremely cooperative. He and Scotty chewed over old times, with Scotty gradually leading him into talk of the Tucker O'Brien case, on which Torgeson had spent countless hours before it was eventually abandoned. Had anything about the case surfaced at this late date that could possibly be tied in with the recent murder of May Minton?

Torgeson laughed off the possibility. He'd heard scuttlebutt that one of the hotshots working out of a midtown precinct was trying to track down the records on the O'Brien murder. Which was laughable, because he and others involved with the case knew those files had mysteriously disappeared some sixteen years ago, just after the case was stamped "CLOSED." Lots of luck.

"Time got away on me," he told Nina. "It was after five by then, and rather than fight the rush-hour crowds, I caught dinner at a little chop house on Forty-seventh Street. I met an old pal and we had a couple of drinks, so I didn't get back to my neighborhood until after nine. I stopped for a nightcap in a local dive about four blocks from my place. By the time I headed home it was after ten-thirty. I was tired, carrying a fair package by then. I guess I wasn't as careful as I might have been."

Apparently someone had been waiting for him, for as Scotty was in the process of crossing the street in front of his building, a car, its lights out, suddenly roared to life, careened from its parking place, and broadsided him.

"There was no other traffic moving on the street, so they weren't avoiding another car. And as proof positive—I hadn't blacked out yet—they backed up, and one guy got out and frisked me. He grabbed the envelope and got away with all the copies I'd made, all my notes. They must have been sure I was dead or they'd probably have put a couple of slugs into me."

"Did you get a look at them?" Nina asked, her voice breathy, edged with tension.

"No way. I was barely breathing."

"The car? Could you describe it?"

"A pile of junk. Maybe a dirty, pale blue. I only got a glimpse of it, just before it rammed me. A Chevy or Dodge sedan, vintage nineteen seventy? Who can tell? Probably stolen. The scuzz most likely ditched it right afterwards. One thing's sure—if we had any cover to

135

speak of, it's gone now." He fixed Nina with a puzzled look. "How do you figure the goons got on me so quick?"

Nina explained that someone at the studio must have overheard her talking to Noel Winston about him, and had taken it from there. "I'm truly sorry, Scotty. It's all my fault. Can you ever forgive me?"

He struggled to bring up a hand and wave off her words. "Forget about it," he mumbled. "You were just trying to find out about your friend. You didn't know what you were up against." He gasped for breath again. "Now you do."

Both fell silent, regarding one another with grave concern. "You're in over your head, Nina," he wheezed finally, "whether you realize it or not. And so am I. These guys are playing hardball." He chuckled hoarsely. "But they don't scare me. I'll be up and around in a few days. And when I am, we'll square things. In for a penny, in for a pound, that's my style. This old newshound's too mean to quit."

He fell into a fresh fit of coughing, and Nina knew she really ought to leave and let him get some rest.

"What about you?" he asked. "You getting anywhere with your snooping?"

"Not really." She told him about last night's frightening delivery, about the less-than-subtle freeze-out at the studio. "What do you make of that?"

"Your cop friend thinks the picture might have come from police files? That's interesting. Could be we have a rogue cop on our hands. Someone on the pad. Is your friend going to check further on this? I sure's hell am, once I get my tail outta here."

"Yes, he's looking into it. Do you think your friend, Lieutenant Torgeson, might be involved?"

Scotty snorted. "Torgie? Hell, no. He's a straight arrow. A bona fide Boy Scout if there ever was one. He'll nose around, too, once he hears about this."

Again Lane fell to coughing. His strength was fading fast. "Which makes me think," he persisted, pleading with his eyes that Nina stay, "that someone out at the precinct could've overheard my line of inquiry. Right away there's a call to his main man. Maybe that's what put the night riders on my tail. It wasn't any of your doing after all, kiddo, so don't blame yourself, okay?"

Nina forced a smile and touched his hand. "Okay. I'll stop and see you again on Saturday, Scotty. You should be ready to go dancing by then."

"Are you offering? Now that's what I call real incentive. It'd be a distinct pleasure, darling, let me tell you. I'd be the envy of every guy in Roseland."

"You rest now, Scotty. Forget the case for now—just get well. And when you do, we've got a date."

His eyes were weary. "Thanks, Nina. I really appreciate your visit. Saturday? That'll give me something to look forward to. Don't forget those photos now."

"Not a chance." And with that, Nina let herself out of the room. A heady resolve and a desire for vengeance formed in her head as she strode down the hospital corridors, her heels clicking on the tile. The dirty creeps, she raged, trying to kill a harmless old man like that! Hardball, was it? She'd show them hardball! Angela, Sylvia, Georgine, the phantom TV network, a crooked cop—whoever is behind this, watch your tail. You'll pay for this. You'll pay in spades!

But not tonight, Nina amended wearily. She was truly beat. She needed a drink, a hot meal, a soak in the tub. She would, just for tonight, try to put all this out of her mind. No call to Rossi, only the most cursory run-through on tomorrow's lines. And early to bed, hopefully to recoup her strength for the grim days that lay ahead.

Chapter Thirteen

It was no use. She'd had the nourishing dinner and a stiff drink, she'd had the relaxing tub, she'd done her homework on the next day's script . . . and she still couldn't sleep. Tossing and turning was not Nina's idea of fun. Finally she hurled off the covers, thrashed her way into her robe, and snapped on the TV.

Seconds later, she was collapsed into a chair, spellbound and thanking the gods of insomnia that they'd worked their magic on her that night. For there, flickering back and forth across her television screen, were three very familiar faces—the Misses Minton, Kastle, and Dyer. Except that the faces weren't really all that familiar, since the movie was about twenty-five years old.

The story was a frothy triangle about three sisters: Harriet (May) was married to Johnnie, yet attracted to Sam, while gaga over Frank; Gloria (Sylvia) was engaged to Sam, yet attracted to Frank, while bananas over Johnnie; and Eve (Georgine) was married to Frank and disgusted by everyone else.

Nina settled into her chair and curled up with Harriet, Gloria, and Eve. Especially Eve. May was wonderful as Harriet, and Sylvia was great as Gloria. But Georgine!! Georgine was something way beyond superb as Eve. She managed to be funny and touching at the same time. She was slim, glamorous, sophisticated, and utterly believable. Although she lacked that indefinable thing called "star quality," she acted rings around both May and Sylvia.

So why, Nina wondered, had she always gotten third billing? Once an actress possesses that ability to create a character and render it with total truthfulness, either on stage or on screen, she doesn't lose it. She can waste it, she can hide it, she can ignore it, but it's always there.

She can hide it. . . .

Nina sat bolt-upright, mental gears smoking. Could it be that Georgine was *still* the supreme actress, and that her third banana status was deliberate? Was the real performance the one she gave *offstage*, the drab and mousey iceberg routine? Something clicked into place in Nina's mind, as it always did when stray facts suddenly fit together and spelled out "truth." Of course, these were exactly the kind of thoughts that Dino would denigrate, but she wouldn't give him a chance. First she'd gather some facts. Some very hard facts.

Without a doubt, Georgine Dyer deserved closer scrutiny.

The scene at the main rehearsal hall on Friday morning was much the same as on Thursday—an unusual number of extras milling around trying to be unobtrusive while also trying to be "discovered." And at the same time they were trying to get as close as they could to Sylvia Kastle and Georgine Dyer, who in turn seemed to be spending as much time as possible in the solitude of their dressing rooms. All in

139

all, less than ideal working conditions at Meyer Studios.

After the lunch break, Nina surveyed the more familiar faces in the hall.

Robin was seated next to Rafe, and judging from their evident coziness they were between lovers' quarrels for once.

Noel Winston was talking to Mary Kennerly. Nina noted that Mary seemed to be guarded about something, while Noel was unusually intense. Check on that one later.

Angela was dancing attendance on Horst, who was lapping it up in an unconcerned sort of way. Nothing peculiar there.

The afternoon lurched along uncomfortably, with results that could only be termed pedestrian. The TTS cast and crew knew themselves well enough to know that the day's episode wouldn't be quite up to their usual standards, and tempers were getting to be very raw around the edges. And on the side, top, bottom, and middle as well.

The only ones who seemed to be having a good time that day were the extras. Some were experienced actors with familiar faces, others were comparative newcomers, but they all needed the work badly. Nina felt a surge of compassion as she watched them. She knew that these little walk-on jobs might be the result of years of effort, and in all likelihood would lead nowhere. But every last one of these people, she was certain, privately nursed the conviction that this could be their big break, that they'd get discovered and be given a line or two to speak, and then be cast in a continuing role.

What a crazy business I'm in, she reflected as Bellamy Carter, one of the assistant directors, walked by.

''Bellamy, you've gone berserk with the background. Were all these people always in the script?'' she asked.

He grimaced. "Not originally. But Horst felt we should pull out all the stops this week. Since we're in the spotlight anyway, we might as well show them how the big boys do it."

"If this is how the big boys do it, you better get somebody to check continuity." Carter seemed puzzled and somewhat offended by Nina's remark. "I didn't see any chauffeurs on the set yesterday."

"You didn't see any kangaroos, either. What are you talking about?" Carter snapped.

"The action in the big scene is continuous, so if you didn't use a chauffeur yesterday, you'd better not use one today."

"Nina, nobody called for a chauffeur."

"Then why do we have one?"

"We don't."

"We do. I saw him two minutes ago."

"Try to understand. *There is no chauffeur* in the script. Look, Nina, we're all a little tired. Why don't you tend to your lines and let me worry about the scenes?"

Nina shrugged. "Don't get so exasperated, Bellamy. If you don't care, why should I?"

But he couldn't let it go. "I don't know—you tell me."

Angela decided to chime in. "Maybe sticking her nose in where it's not needed has become such a habit she can't break it." Other people were listening by now.

Nina put her script down and stood up. "Angela, that was not necessary. All I'm saying is that one of the extras is wearing a chauffeur's uniform, and by the way, it's a lousy fit! Now if that's all right with Bellamy, it's all right with me!"

141

"It's fine with me!" Carter stated between clenched teeth.

"Great." Oh God, this was all so idiotic.

"What is this, a stress test?" Carter asked.

"What are they arguing about?" Spence called.

Angela explained the contretemps, and was rewarded with a peal of derisive laughter from Sylvia, who had just arrived.

"If Miss McFall says she saw a chauffeur, then she probably did," she said in a maddeningly condescending way. "It was most likely *my* chauffeur." Somehow her tone implied that of course everyone, including the extras, had uniformed chauffeurs waiting for them.

"Since when are outsiders allowed on the set?" Nina asked Spence.

Sylvia's back stiffened and she dropped the amused tone. "Some of us have certain privileges, and others don't. Can we get on with this?"

As the final taping began, Nina was grateful that none of her scenes were with either Angela or Sylvia.

Before leaving the studio late in the afternoon, Nina called Dino at the precinct. Despite her resolve about gathering nothing but hard facts, she wanted to share her thoughts about Georgine Dyer that last night's old movie had generated. But she never got to it.

"Can't talk to you now, babe," Dino said brusquely. "Possible break to follow up. We got a report from Maine. You know—where Minton's nephew lives?"

"Yes?"

"The guy is deep in debt. . . ."

"You called that one."

142

"And he and his wife haven't been seen for over a week. They got into their jalopy and vanished two days before May Minton was killed."

Good Lord, not another suspect! "Dino," Nina began, "doesn't it seem to you that the answer lies closer to home?"

"You may be right. Then again, you may be wrong. In the meantime, I'm following up on the nephew. Talk to you later, babe. And don't take any chances, hear?"

Nina sighed. "Not a one."

As Nina hung up, she decided that if Dino wanted to waste time with a wild lobster chase in Maine, that was his business. She had other fish to fry.

Chapter Fourteen

Nina arrived at the hospital Saturday shortly after two, her arms loaded with gifts. She couldn't help but notice that there were no cards, no plants, no sign of other visitors; it was evident that Scotty Lane had no relatives or close friends. Or if he did, they hadn't as yet learned of his accident.

"Nina," he said, "if you ain't a sight for sore eyes." He appraised her smart, black wool Chanel suit, her dark hose, the gleaming pumps. "They're just making 'em better every year. Beautiful. You must have to fight the guys off with a club."

"Keep it up," she laughed, busily arranging a bouquet of cut flowers in a vase she'd brought along and putting a chrysanthemum plant on the window where the sun set the golden blooms on fire. "Flattery will get you anywhere." She paused, looked down on him approvingly. "Oh, Scotty, you're looking one hundred percent better."

"Thanks, beautiful. I'm doing okay. I'm gonna be here a while yet. They keep finding new things wrong. I got broken bones where I didn't even know I had bones." He grimaced. "Ooh. That one got me. Only hurts when I laugh."

"*Voilà!*" Nina exclaimed, opening a brown envelope and spreading a dozen publicity photos of herself across the foot of the bed. "That ought to hold you. I brought my pen. I can autograph into the wee hours."

Next she presented him with two gift-wrapped boxes, one containing a new necktie, the other a Gucci wallet. "I had no idea what you needed, Scotty. Just something to let you know I'm truly sorry about all the trouble I got you into."

His eyes filled with emotion. "Dammit, you didn't have to do anything like that. Just your coming to see me would have been enough. Thanks." His mouth twisted into a sly grin. "I don't suppose you brought any cigarettes along?"

"Sorry, but no," Nina said, "I don't smoke."

"Ah!" he snorted. "What the hell! It's a filthy habit. I know I gotta quit. Forget I mentioned it." Again he beamed. "Lord, if you aren't the prettiest thing."

"Please. You're embarrassing me."

"Did you notice the hospital staff giving you the eye when you came through?"

"Well, now that you mention it, there *were* a lot of smiling faces in the corridors. What's it all about?"

"One of the nurses got a fix on you the other day. Word got around. Big soap opera star. Now I'm a celebrity, too, because I know you. Such service you never saw. You don't realize how much joy you bring into people's lives, kid. Especially mine."

"Stop it, now. You want me ruining my mascara?"

"Hell, that would never do, would it? Anyway, it's wonderful to see you. How's the Minton caper coming along?"

Nina instantly became serious. "Not too well, I'm afraid. I really threw a monkey wrench into things yesterday."

"How so? Drag up a chair, tell me about it."

Nina did, relieved to tell her troubles to someone else, and at the same time feeling a large sense of guilt

145

that she was telling Scotty when she hadn't, as yet, breathed a word to Rossi.

She started at the very beginning, brushing in her growing antagonism with Sylvia and her curiosity about Georgine's dried prune act, and ending with yesterday's studio events.

"You and this cop pal of yours getting any closer to a motive?" Scotty asked.

"Not really. His name's Dino Rossi, by the way. You'll be meeting him eventually. I haven't told him about you."

"Oh? How come?"

Nina paused. "It's hard to say. It's just that there are times when I don't share everything with him. He's got his own ideas about the case, and he tends to put me down at times. He doesn't always take me seriously."

"I know the feeling," Scotty said.

"Anyway, Dino gets in a rut, and nobody can budge him. He's in a rut right now, so I'm just backing off, putting out feelers of my own. I'm trying to make things happen, to force the issue. Do you know what I'm trying to say?"

"Sure I do. You're an independent, feisty broad. And you want people to give you your head, even if it might be on a platter."

Nina grimaced. "You have a very colorful way with words, Scotty."

"The question was motive. Does this Rossi guy have a glimmer?"

Nina felt a definite twinge of disloyalty as she said, "Not really. In fact he's still half-convinced that Angela's our target."

"And you have a different theory?"

"Yes, of course. Something's in the wind, something to do with Tucker O'Brien's murder, but in an oblique way. It's as though that murder has come back

146

to haunt someone. I told this to Dino, but he didn't quite buy it. What I figure is that when May was invited to come on the show, she must have spilled *something* to Helen Meyer or Horst Krueger or somebody."

"What kind of something?"

"That's the sticker. Whatever it was, it got around and set someone off."

"And how're you and this Rossi guy going to find out what it was?"

"We're working on that. Dino's questioning Helen Meyer and Horst Krueger some time today."

Scotty suggested, "Maybe he should put Georgine and Sylvia under the light, too. And while he's at it, how about setting up a seance and just ask May a couple of direct questions? You know how she loved to gab."

Nina laughed, thankful for the break in tension. "Oh, you're good for me, Scotty. I think we're going to be seeing a lot of each other in the future."

"I certainly hope so. We still have that date at Roseland, remember?"

"How could I forget?" Nina gathered up the photographs and got out her pen. "How would you like these inscribed?"

"Seriously, Nina," he stalled, "I'm impressed. It sounds to me like you've done your homework, like you're both approaching this in a very thorough way. Keep digging. Someone's bound to let something slip. One thread at a time—that's how mysteries are solved." He broke into a fit of coughing. "And in the meantime, I'll keep thinking. I have a phone, there are some people I might call. Time is one thing I've got plenty of."

"About these photos, Scotty—I've got to run. Big date tonight. Tell me what to write."

"Somebody's beating my time already? Who, Rossi?"

"My, Grandpa, what big eyes you have!"

"Reporters. We have a sixth sense. Besides, *your* eyes are a dead giveaway. Every time you say his name—even when you're running the guy down."

Nina let that pass without comment. She sat upright, poised her pen. " 'To Scotty,' " she read aloud as she wrote, " 'my sweetheart forever. With enduring love, Nina.' Does that sound okay?"

"C'mon. You wanna cause a heart attack here and now?"

She grinned and passed the photo to him. "Now, who else?"

He smiled embarrassedly. "Well, if it wouldn't be too much trouble, a couple of the nurses been asking. Let's see, there's Virginia and Kelly and . . ."

Nina and Rossi were again at Ernie's Steakhouse, a favorite eating place for cops working the uptown precincts. Tonight Nina was wearing a two-piece gray and white jacquard dress with a scoop neckline and a modified peplum, very demure. Her red hair was piled high on her head, and a pearl choker accented her exquisite throat.

Dinner was over, and they were coasting before returning to Nina's apartment, each of them nursing a Drambuie. During dinner, deliberately postponing their conversation about the Minton case, he'd launched into an anecdote about Peter's escapades.

At last Nina said, "What about our case? Judging from the way you've avoided the subject all evening, the news can't be good."

Rossi lowered his eyes, drumming the table top with long, tapered fingers. "No, not good at all."

"Tell me."

"Dead end at ever turn. Minton's nephew still hasn't turned up. We put out an APB on him. And the TV network lead fizzled. Nothing at all there that would tie in with Miss Minton's murder. They tripled Meyer Productions' offer, and May turned them down." He gazed at Nina intently. "And you know why?"

"No, why?"

"Because May's good friend, Nina McFall, worked for Meyer Productions, so she wanted to be with that company. They had no way of combatting that, so that angle went belly-up. Same with Helen Meyer."

Nina came alert. "What did she say?"

"She gave me her usual lady-of-the-manor act. Delighted to be interviewed. I got absolutely nothing out of her. She didn't remember anything untoward that May might have said during any of their sessions. I came at her six ways from Sunday, and never got close to anything we could use." Dino paused, then said, "Is she playing with a full deck? Does she see herself as some kind of a sex object or something?"

Nina rolled her eyes. "Don't tell me Helen made a pass at you! Did she offer you lunch, a drink? A tour of the house? To see her new bedroom drapes perhaps?"

"Nina!" Rossi rebuked. "What a thing to say. She's an old woman."

"So? Old women need love, too." She covered her mouth with her hand to conceal a smile. "You stingy thing!"

Dino flushed and looked away, obviously embarrassed. "Anyway, no leads there. Nor from Horst Krueger, although he admitted he didn't attend all the meetings. He led me to believe that Helen was really the powerhouse behind snagging May Minton for the show."

"That leaves Angela Dolan, then. You still think she's the kingpin in the case?"

Rossi rubbed his head impatiently. "I don't know

149

what I think anymore," he fumed. "There are times when I could pitch the whole damned thing, go peddle windups on Fifth Avenue."

"Let's," Nina said. "We'll be raggle-taggle gypsies."

Dino grinned at her. "Nina, you are such a nut! God, if I didn't have you . . ."

Their eyes locked. Their fingers twined. Nina said softly, "Dino, I love you. When we get back to my apartment, I'll show you how much."

Dino regained his composure, and forced himself to concentrate on business. "So where do we go from here? Dolan? Winston? Mysterious nephew? We checked that visitor's register at Carson Place backward and forward. Zilch. How May's murderer got up to her apartment I'll never understand. That bugs the hell out of me!"

Nina's fingers tightened on his. "It'll come. Give it time."

"Time! We don't have any time. Every day we delay means there's that much less chance of cracking this thing." He glanced at her. "What's new in your territory? Anything happening I should know about?"

"I thought you'd never ask," she said. "Oh yes. I've got quite a story to tell."

After she finished her account of Scotty Lane's "accident" and her hospital visits, she told him her thoughts about both Sylvia and Georgine.

"Wow," he said finally, "sounds like you've had your hands full." She didn't like the pained overtones in his voice.

"What do you think, Dino? Am I doing the right things?" she asked anxiously.

He avoided her eyes, toyed with his Drambuie. "Well, to be perfectly frank, I wouldn't have handled it that way."

"But you're not perfectly Frank," she said, trying

150

to suppress a swell of resentment by teasing him. "You're perfectly Dino." A raised eyebrow was all she got for that, and more than she deserved. "So you think I'm fouling things up?"

"I didn't say that. I just meant I'd approach things differently."

"How would you have handled the thing with Scotty Lane?"

"Well," he began slowly, "for starters, you could have checked with me to see if I knew anything about the guy. Just because you got his name from Noel Winston doesn't mean he was automatically clean."

Nina frowned. "You know, Dino, it's starting to sound to me as though the very name of Noel Winston puts your teeth on edge."

"Any friend of Noel's is a friend of yours?"

"Yes, something like that. Why not? Don't you have any friends you trust to that extent?"

"Trust doesn't play a very big part in my scheme of things."

"Well, you'd better realize that it plays a lead role in mine!"

"Are you hearing this, Nina? We're deep in the big muddy. I did ask you to back off the other night, didn't I? But you wouldn't listen."

The mellow mood of moments before had swiftly faded. Nina's eyes flared. "I told you I wasn't going to lay off. I told you I have an even bigger stake in this case than you do. And that's all you can say, that you would have handled things differently? You don't care at all that this sweet old man who was trying to help me almost got *killed*? God, but you can be so arrogant, so bullheaded sometimes!"

"Please, Nina. Lower your voice. People are staring."

"Let them stare!" She stood up. "Let them stare at me walking out of this place! *Without you!*" She picked

151

up her handbag and began stalking out of the restaurant.

Dino caught her at the door. "At least wait until I pay the check, for Christ's sake!"

"Don't you curse at me, and don't put yourself out on my account. I'm still able to call a cab, even though I'm only a stupid, blundering woman."

"Dammit, be reasonable, will you? Stay where you are. You'll go home in my car, understand?"

They didn't speak all the way to her apartment. And when Rossi tried to find a parking place near the main entrance, she told him not to bother.

"Nina, listen. I didn't mean it that way at all," Dino began. "We've got to talk. We've got to straighten things out between us. I—"

"I said don't bother. Please let me off at the door."

His temper exploded just then. "All right!" he stormed. "Be that way. I'm too tired to play childish games. Good night!"

Nina flounced from the car, ran past Willie, and headed straight for the elevator.

As she stabbed at the door lock with her key, her eyes blurry with tears, it suddenly dawned on her—the most monumental of realizations—she and Dino had just had their first serious fight.

Chapter Fifteen

Monday morning, shortly after 8:30 A.M., Angela Dolan threw her semiannual tantrum. With the entire cast, the floor writers, the director and assistant directors on hand, she blew her stack. Short and simple: She was being shortchanged in the newest rewrites and she wasn't going to take it anymore. For the cast newcomers and the extras, it was a classic display of prima donna pique.

The offending scene revolved around some humorous business between Angela and the Zane sisters. The trouble, according to Angela, was that there wasn't as much business for Angela as for Georgine and Sylvia. And when Mark Viner, a mere dialogue writer, presumed to address her complaint, she officiously cut him off.

"That will do, Mr. Viner," she shouted. "When I want to talk to the hired help, I'll let you know. This is between Sally and me." Sally Burman was the second writer, now assigned to the set instead of working with Dave Gelber and his crew situated in the specially established studio at Leatherwing, the Meyer estate. "What about this, Sally?" she stormed. "I spent all weekend learning these lines, and now when I get here I find everything changed, and *my* part cut to ribbons. How do you expect any-one to work under conditions like these?''

"Don't blow your stack, Angela," said Sally, a considerable voice in her own right. "What lines are you talking about? What page?"

"The page we're running," Angela spat, treating Sally like a backward child, "what else? I had that long monologue where I explained city mouse, country mouse to Sylvia and Georgine. I had pre-pared it, worked on it, *conquered* it; I was ready to really breathe some *life* into the sterile pap you and Dave have been dishing up for us lately."

It was Sally's turn to be patronizing. "It had to be cut, Angela. Surely you, as an *old-time* profes-sional can see that. The scene was draggy as hell. You'll have to agree the pace is much improved."

"I'll agree with nothing!" Angela stormed. "If the scene was running long, then you should have seen that when you were writing it, not after I've spent all weekend memorizing this drivel!"

"C'mon now, Angela," Spence Sprague inter-vened, "knock it off. If you've got a gripe, air it at a cast meeting. This isn't the place for it. We're on schedule here, we—"

"Then we'll just be *off* schedule, won't we?" An-gela hissed. "It's time we faced up to this kind of incompetence. These *exalted* writers of ours seem to think that we acting peons have no rights whatso-ever. I'm here to say different."

"*Mea culpa.*" Sally made a mock show of beating her breast. "*Mea maxima culpa.* We've still only got a half hour for this show. It *is The Turning Seasons*, remember, not an Angela Dolan retrospective."

The dig wasn't lost on Angela. "Retrospective, is it?" she shrieked. She actually threw her script at Sally. "Here's *retrospective* for you!" She whirled, started for the door. "When you've reinstated my

154

lines as I learned them, call me! I'll be in my dressing room!" She paused dramatically, fixing Sprague with a vindictive glare. "So much for your damned schedule," she snapped, knowing full well she had him over a barrel. Then she turned on her heel and stalked out of the studio.

Immediately the main rehearsal hall became a buzzing beehive. Sally Burman shifted from one foot to the other, as though she were dancing on a hot griddle. Spencer Sprague lowered his head like a charging bull and went after Angela. The cast members quickly broke into small groups, everyone grumbling full tilt.

"There goes the morning," Robin Tally sighed to Nina. "We'll never get caught up."

"It'll blow over," Nina said, deliberately ignoring the furor. "It always does. Give Angela ten minutes. She'll come down like a lamb. It's something she has to get out of her system every once in a while."

"You're certainly taking it calmly," Robin said.

Nina shrugged. "Worse things could happen."

"Judging from the way you look this morning, they already have."

"No comment. Concentrate on Angela. Leave me out of this, will you?"

"Grrr," Robin said as she got up and moved to join Rafe Fallone. "Looks like it's gonna be one of those days."

Nina pretended to study her lines. She didn't feel like talking to anyone this morning.

Dino hadn't called on Sunday. She'd stayed up late, hoping that Rossi, lonely and contrite, would break down at the last moment and call, but her phone might as well have been cast in bronze.

Whatever had gotten into her Saturday night? And into Rossi as well? One moment things had

155

been going swimmingly, with a beautiful buildup to a night of ecstasy. And the next, World War III. What had set them off?

Foolish question. She and Dino had a fundamental and profound difference of opinion on the role of the sexes. They would always have this problem, and Nina knew she had two choices: Either learn to compromise and roll with things when Dino's chauvinism became insufferable, or . . .

She dreaded even to consider what her life would be without Dino. Her gloomy, solitary Sunday had given her an unwelcome preview.

Why not just get out of the detective business? she asked herself. It was a tempting thought. Did she really need all this—the worry, the fear, the sleepless nights? Things like the photo she'd received Wednesday night? Like the threat that was implicit in Scotty Lane's hit-and-run?

But she knew, deep down, that it was too late to turn back now. She was deeply committed to helping Dino solve the crime.

She owed it to Scotty. And she owed it to May; despite the unsavory details revealed since her death, May had been Nina's friend. She had held Nina in high esteem. Wasn't it only fitting she honor that regard by finding out who killed May?

The determination she'd felt on Saturday after seeing Scotty in the hospital came flooding back. Without a doubt, she'd get to the bottom of this thing—with or without Mr. Goddamn Dino Detectivce-Lieutenant Rossi!

But all the same, she wanted so much to hear his voice. . . .

After ten minutes, Nina, seeing that she was getting nowhere with her lines, decided to put her time to more productive use. Yesterday, while studying the script, she'd come upon some confusing stage business in Melanie Prescott's office. How was she going to bring that off? Maybe it would be a good idea to wander out to the soundstage, walk through it on the set itself.

When last we saw Melanie Prescott, female business tycoon, Nina parodied as she slipped unnoticed from the rehearsal room. That burglary scene the Zane sisters and I had discovered upon entering, with drawers pulled out and papers scattered all over, had been a mess. *Today we find Melanie Prescott,* the script read, *picking up things in her usually immaculate office.* By all means, she thought, feeling her way down the aisle between the rows of half-sets, let's get a jump on things.

The floods and arcs were off; the dimly glowing overheads turned the miniature world of Kingston Falls into a deserted, eerie ghost town. The production crews on break and a couple of gaffers at the far end manhandling a flat into place were the only other human beings in sight. As Nina felt her way in the gloom, she was stabbed by a distinct sense of vulnerability. All alone, her departure not seen, she was a sitting duck, should there be anyone lurking in the shadows.

Will you knock off that stuff? she scolded. Even so, remembering the incident of the falling steel, she looked warily left and right.

Upon reaching Melanie Prescott's office, she regarded the fallout from Friday's segment. The mess had been left on purpose, part of Monday's continuing action. Even in the muted light, she could still see well enough to read the script, plan her moves.

According to the stage directions Melanie would be kneeling on the carpet, reaching beneath the couch for sheets of paper when the scene opened. Nina knelt, executed sham pick-up movements, all the while adjusting for the most advantageous camera angles. Now, still kneeling, she came upright, consulted the script again.

Next Melanie moves across the room, straightens the shade on the lamp in the corner. She faked that motion, leaving the shade askew, of course. *She stares down at the top of her desk, surveying the drawers, most of them still open. She leans to recover a vital file.*

It was here, staring past the file folder, that Nina saw something odd. Where did that cable come from? she wondered. I never noticed it before. What's it for?

Again she dropped to all fours and peered beneath her desk, a steel monstrosity that the property man had acquired at a salvage outlet. She wanted to get a better view of the line where it snaked behind the desk. Granted, the sets were always crawling with cables, and it was a constant chore to avoid tripping over them.

But Nina was certain this particular cable hadn't been there on Friday. What new connection had the head electrician authorized over the weekend? Damn it, someone has to warn the actors when new hazards are going to be placed in their paths.

Instinctively she recoiled and began to move away from the desk. The hairs on the back of her neck stiffened; her spine seemed to melt. Dear God! Could it be? Were they ready to go that far? She found herself gasping for breath.

Inch by inch, terrified, she crawled away from the desk. When she was sure she was far enough from it, trembling, she rose to her feet. Still keeping her eyes fixed on the desk, almost as if she were afraid it would roll forward and attack her, she removed the heavy steel spring clip she used for a placemarker from the edge of her script.

Her breath clogging her throat, she poised the clip in her palm, then gently lofted it toward the metal

urface, aiming for a bare space just to the left of the
blotter.

She jumped back at the crisp explosion, as a
blinding white arc of light sparked across the desk's
urface. A cloud of acrid smoke assailed her nostrils.
Nina screamed.

At the same time, the overhead lights went out
and the entire area of the soundstage where she
tood was plunged into darkness. Nina shrieked
again.

Seconds later she heard shouts and the sound of
unning feet. She saw someone loping toward her,
he beam of a flashlight cutting wild patterns
hrough the gloom. The glaring light picked her up.

"Are you all right, Ms. McFall?" It was Arnie
Nelson, the chief electrician. "What happened?"

Nina forced herself to speak. "I—I think someone
ust tried to kill me."

"My God! How?"

"That desk. It's rigged. Someone meant to elec-
rocute me. Don't touch it!"

"The harm's been done, Ms. McFall. Whatever
you did, it shorted the circuit, threw out a breaker."
He deliberately placed his hand on the steel surface.
"See, power's out. Here, let me take a look." He
dropped to his knees, crawled behind the desk.

"Well, I'll be damned," he exclaimed. "This baby's hooked up just like an electric chair. There's at
east two-twenty coming in here. You'd have fried,
sure as hell."

Nina swayed in place, fought pangs of nausea. If
I hadn't come out here just now, if I'd have waited
for the actual walkthrough—*I never would have seen
hat cable! They'd have got me for sure!*

Abruptly Nelson was up and running out of the
half-set. Now his light bobbed behind the walls. By
hen another man, his assistant, came running up.

159

"Get that circuit breaker," Arnie ordered. "We're clear here."

Shortly the lights came up, and more members of the production crew gathered around Nina protectively. "You okay, Nina?" "You sure?" "What happened?"

"I disconnected it at the main trunk," Nelson assured them, again dropping behind the desk. This time he reappeared with the mutilated cable. "See?" he said excitedly. "One of the lines was cut, and the two bare ends were taped to each of the back legs of the desk. Just like an electric cattle fence. But with two-twenty volts going through it, it would have killed the whole herd."

Not thinking clearly, her whole body trembling, Nina said, "Fun and games, Arnie? Is this your idea of a joke?"

His eyebrows shot up. "Not me, Ms. McFall! Nobody here did this. This is no joke, you know. Somebody was playing for keeps, and no mistake."

Moments later Spence Sprague appeared. "Keep the rest of those people out of here, Arnie," he ordered. "And everybody keep your mouth shut about this. The less said, the better, understand?" He waved the curious crew away, then put his arm around Nina and led her to the couch. "Now, tell me, Nina. Just what in hell's going on here? Has the whole world gone crazy?"

She was still trembling when she finished telling him what had happened, touching briefly—and reluctantly—on the possible reasons why someone might want to electrocute her. "Dear Lord," she gasped, still stunned by this latest brush with death, "it could have been anyone, not just me. Whoever touched that desk first."

"What kind of animal would do that?" Sprague wondered aloud.

160

That did it. Nina jerked to her feet and made a statement that caused Sprague to stare at her in amazement. "I don't know. But I'm going to find out if it kills me!"

"What's the matter with you, Nina?" he asked quietly. "Wasn't once enough? You have to keep coming back for seconds? When are you gonna be satisfied with just being a damned actress?"

Chapter Sixteen

Later that afternoon, way behind schedule, they finally reached the end of the day's run-through and Spence Sprague gave the cast a much-needed break. "That wasn't so much a run-through as a stumble-through," he grumbled. "Dress rehearsal in twenty minutes."

Nina had recovered some of her composure after a brief but intense case of the shakes, but she knew she was still a long way from giving a convincing performance. The morning's incident had cast a pall over everyone, and even the most battle-scarred members of the cast were doing little more than walking through their roles.

Aware that her attitude was affecting everyone and that she could make or break the day's taping, Nina settled into a corner of the main rehearsal hall and dug deep into reserves she could only hope and pray were there. She was helped through the challenge by two events. The first came from an unexpected source: Helen Meyer.

"Surprise, surprise," she said as she passed out a handful of formal-looking envelopes to the cast principals. "I was saving these for the end of the

162

day, but I think we could all use a little boost right about now."

The envelopes contained invitations to a dinner party that Saturday evening at the palatial Meyer estate, Leatherwing, in honor of Miss Kastle and Miss Dyer. Without a doubt, Helen was correct in predicting the cast's reactions; everyone was delighted. Helen Meyer, regardless of her faults as an employer, was a peerless hostess, and visions of a lavish dinner and a fountain of vintage wines helped considerably in improving the general mood.

The second event that got Nina through the rest of the day was the fact that Dino called just before the dress rehearsal got under way. Before he had a chance to say anything, Nina poured out a description of the morning's events.

"Who could have done it?" he muttered. "Who had access to the studio over the weekend? That's when the wiring job on your desk must have taken place. That settles it—I'm calling Angela Dolan in."

"Today wouldn't be good," Nina said ruefully. "She's been on one mighty tear all day. And we're an hour behind schedule as it is. She'd eat you alive." She proceeded to sketch in the details of Dolan's tantrum. "Besides, what does she know about electricity?"

"Money talks. She could have hired someone." But he seemed to doubt that himself. "Okay, I'll just drop in unexpectedly tomorrow. Maybe that'll jar her a bit."

"I'm sure it will. But please, be discreet, will you?"

"It won't be easy. Considering my outrage over the fact that she's just tried to do you in, I'd like to strangle her with my bare hands."

"Hardly an objective attitude, is it?" she teased. "What does your detective manual say about 'dispassionate interrogation?' '' He ignored the question.

"I don't suppose it would do any good to send some of my men over to look for fingerprints. What about that desk?''

"The electrician had his hands all over it before I thought about prints,'' Nina told him.

"I think I'll send Paul over there just the same. Tell everyone, hands off.''

"I'll do my best. But we finally did the run-through and we're going to start the dress any minute now. I have to go. I'll call you later.''

It wasn't much of a conversation, but it made all the difference for Nina in wrestling with her immediate problem. The thaw had set in, the ice was melting.

At 3:00 P.M., when they should have been halfway through final taping, they had only just finished the dress rehearsal. Nina grabbed the chance to call Dino back.

They exchanged apologies for the fight on Saturday evening and agreed to talk in person and iron out their disagreements.

"Look, if it wasn't Angela,'' Dino persisted in an abrupt change of topic, "then who could it have been?''

"Good question. I just can't come up with anything. It certainly wasn't done this morning; there wasn't time. Someone had to have come in on Saturday or Sunday when nobody else was around. They set it up, and left it. The minute Arnie switched on the main power this morning, the trap went live.''

"What about Sylvia or Georgine? Could they get

in?'' Rossi asked. ''Without being seen by security?''

''It's a puzzler, Dino. Right now I can't even begin to think straight. But there's an explanation, I'm sure.'' She paused. ''And as if all this excitement isn't enough . . .'' She told him about Helen's dinner party plans.

''At Leatherwing?'' His voice was incredulous. ''I'd think, after what happened at her last party, that she'd be spooked for life. Are you going?''

''I'm thinking about it.''

''Seems to me that I once heard a beautiful redhead I know vowing that she'd never set foot in that place again as long as she lived.''

''This is different. What if something happened out there, if a vital clue surfaced, and I wasn't there? I'd never forgive myself. As much as I hate the thought of going back there, I just can't see how I can avoid it.''

''Well this time you don't go alone, understand? Every time I think of how close I came to losing you. I still have nightmares.''

''That's not necessary. I'm not a child, after all.''

''You weren't a child when Byron Meyer got to you, either. And look what nearly happened.'' They were edging too close to dangerous ground again.

''Dino, can't we talk about this later?''

''I guess we can. Anyway, right now I'm going over to Carson Place. I intend to comb through that guest register one more time.''

Nina heard her name on the public-address system. ''Oops. They're calling for me. I have to go. Take care, Dino.''

The day wound to a maddening, bone-wearying close. Nina had never been so happy to see the inviting confines of her apartment as she was that evening.

* * *

Nina was written out of the TTS script on Tuesday. Good thing, because she was on the raw edge of things; she needed time to regroup. The last attempt on her life had taken its toll; she was definitely burned out.

Her afternoon visit with Scotty Lane helped somewhat. He was much improved, his mere spirits high, and he was looking forward to being released from the hospital by the end of the following week.

Nina was not the best of company, despite the fact that Scotty joshed nonstop in an attempt to temper her dark mood.

They talked around all possible angles of the latest attempt on Nina's life. Was it Angela? Were Nina's theories off base? Had Angela—or Sylvia—realized the script's potential and seen Monday morning's scene as a perfect place to end Nina's meddling once and for all? Either woman was capable of recruiting some unsavory flunky to do the actual dirty work. Angela could get someone from the studio production staff proper; she knew where the weak links might be. And Sylvia? She could probably get her chauffeur to do it. He looked the type. Right out of central casting.

At the end she and Scotty were no further along than when they'd started.

"You wait for me now, Nina," Scotty Lane said gruffly as she stood up to leave. "Just lay back for a few days. And when I get outta this damned place . . . Those creeps'll never know what hit 'em."

On the way home she remembered Dino's remark of yesterday about his continuing concern with the mystery of how May's murderer had penetrated the Carson Place security system. She had given it extra thought, and she, too, was mystified by the puzzle.

She'd be passing within striking distance of the place on her way and she had the time to spare . . .

She was disappointed to see that Sam Nastasi, the security guard who'd been on duty the last time, was not behind the desk. She moved into a corner of the glass and steel lobby, sat on a leather-upholstered bench, and quietly watched the comings and goings of the ultrawealthy. Perhaps the mouse-in-the-corner approach would serve to spark some long-quiescent synapses in her brain, conjure up a breakthrough thought.

She sat there for perhaps ten minutes, watching people come and go. But she found her mind wandering, inspecting instead the clothing of the women, pondering the occupations of the men. This wasn't what she'd come for at all.

A woman of Nina McFall's beauty and bearing cannot remain anonymous for very long. The security person, a bright-eyed, smiling, balding rolypoly, kept glancing in her direction. Finally he walked over. "Pardon me, ma'am," he said, "but is there something I could help you with? Are you waiting for someone?"

Nina was equal to the moment. "Mr. Nastasi. Doesn't he work here anymore?"

"Sam? Oh, sure, he's still with us. He called in sick this morning. I'm just filling in for him today. You want I should give you his number or something?"

"No, that won't be necessary. It's just that he was here the other day when I called. I thought I'd say hello." Her mind raced. She had asked Dino specifically about Nastasi and had been assured that his testimony had checked out; nothing in the interrogation had given Dino cause to believe that Nastasi had been paid to look the other way, or to lie about May Minton's callers.

"Oh, you were here the other day?" the man asked. "Who did you come to see? If I'd been on duty, I would have remembered you because you're not one of our residents."

"No, I'm not a resident. I was here to see Miss Minton. It was the day she was murdered."

The man flinched. "Oh," he said after a long pause. "Yeah. Bad news, that day."

And then, at that moment, a connection was made inside Nina's skull. The man had said, "I would have remembered you because you're not one of our residents." She moved backward a step, as if someone had just hit her in the stomach. Of course, she exulted, wanting to exclaim aloud. If you were one of our residents, she elaborated, putting herself in the guard's place, I would have taken it in stride. I wouldn't have asked any questions about who you were or where you were going.

She resisted the impulse to slap her palm against her forehead. Of course! That's it! Why didn't I see it before?

"Please, would you ask Mr. Maxey to come down? Tell him it's Nina McFall. He'll remember me, I'm sure."

Instantly the guard's eyes became apprehensive. What had he done wrong? Had he overstepped himself? Was this super-elegant woman going to cause trouble? "Yes, ma'am," he muttered, moving quickly to his station, where he tapped out the in-house number.

"Miss McFall," Ronald Maxey greeted her when he appeared four minutes later, sham delight in his gaze. "How nice to see you again. Whatever brings you here today?"

"More detective work, Mr. Maxey," she said, noticing the minor chagrin that transformed his smile.

168

"Still trying to find out how someone got up to Miss Minton's apartment without being observed."

"Oh? And how may I help you today?"

"Would you please call up the guest register on that computer of yours," she said crisply, her gaze never wavering, "and check to see if you have either a Lance Kirby or an Earnest Claypool listed among your residents?"

He sent a quirky, patronizing smile, then dutifully began punching the computer keys.

"No, I'm afraid not," he said a moment later. "No one here by those names."

"Please?" she said, moving close, her disappointment crushing. "May I see?"

It was as he'd said. No Claypool in the Cs. No Kirby in the Ks. She was just turning away, in the process of expelling an exasperated sigh, when her eye caught a listing two spaces above. Her heart seemed to leap into her throat. Kirbonsyzk Enterprises? Dear God, it couldn't be! What had Scotty called him? Carbon Six?

"Who is this?" she demanded. "Do you have any information on this tenant?"

Maxey sent her an angry look. "The Kirbonsyzk apartment is our premiere residence. The man who built Carson Place occupies it whenever he's in the city. He and his wife have a country home somewhere on Long Island."

"Oh, is that so?" Nina responded, hard put to keep the excitement out of her voice. "Interesting." Good Lord, talk about lucky breaks!

"Yes," he went on, "they've kept the apartment here ever since the building opened. Says a lot for a building when the builder thinks enough of it to live in it—even part of the time."

Nina wanted to let out a victory whoop.

Chapter Seventeen

It was Saturday afternoon. Four days had passed without further developments, and as Nina selected her clothes for Helen's dinner party that night at Leatherwing, she wrestled with a very guilty conscience.

Why haven't you told Dino, she asked herself for the thousandth time since Tuesday's discovery of the Kirby-Kastle-Kirbonsyzk apartment at Carson Place? Are you on another ego trip? Is pride going to goeth before you fall on your well-paid face?

Maybe so. Nina admitted to herself that she wanted to prove to Dino Rossi that a woman could cut it in the dangerous so-called man's world. And she knew, too, that she was angry at his condescending attitude, the way he treated her like a child at times. His long-suffering sneering at some of her theories was unbearable. Okay, maybe some of them were a little extreme, even wild, but his admiration for her good ideas was grudging at best, almost as though he felt required to pay her occasional lip service just to calm her down.

She had firmly intended to call Rossi again and tell him about Kirby's Carson Place apartment the minute she got home on Tuesday. But then, at the last moment, she changed her mind. Not now, she rationalized. Sleep on it. Enjoy your moment of vindication a little longer. Savor it, wallow in it. Wednesday morning was soon enough. She'd call during her first break, arrange for lunch, a strategy session.

But Wednesday brought another crisis on the TTS set (or so she'd managed to convince herself) and the day passed without the call being placed.

Then, Wednesday night, when he called, very discouraged to relay the results of his interview with Angela Dolan, she'd still kept her silence, even though it would have been the ideal moment.

"Zilch," he admitted disgustedly. "She's got an ironclad alibi. Drove over to Newark to visit an aunt who's dying of cancer. The whole family was there. I called a couple of relatives; her story checks. There's no way she could have been at Minton's apartment that afternoon."

Now, she told herself, tell him now. That we've got that conniving harpy cold. There's no way Sylvia will be able to weasel out of it. Just watch her face when you accuse her. She'll fold up like a concertina.

But again, she'd held back. Because, in the darkest depths of her psyche, that's exactly what she intended to do herself. She wanted to face down Sylvia Kastle the first moment she caught her off guard and accuse her point-blank. Singlehandedly, spurning any male backup whatsoever. And if Sylvia pulled her gracious-lady act, she'd lay it all on the line. She'd slam her right between her vapid, blue eyes with the damning discovery of the Kirbonsyzk apartment. Which would either put Sylvia down for the count or drive her to do something foolish, something incriminatingly desperate. But when? Who knows, maybe even tonight at Helen's

171

party. She'd recognize the appropriate moment when she saw it.

As for Rossi, he'd called last night offering to accompany her to Leatherwing this evening; he would wait in the car all evening long to make sure nothing happened to her. But Nina had talked him out of the notion, promising to call him when she returned, and to fill him in on the complete developments Sunday at lunch. The day would be his. They'd finally have their long overdue heart-to-heart. And she was so sorry that her week had been so hectic, that there hadn't been time before now. It would be special, she promised.

"And how," she demanded of her hair dryer, "how will you explain your duplicity to him then, after the fact?" The hair dryer was as talkative as the shower had been. "You'll just have to cross that bridge when you come to it. After all, shouldn't he be delighted when you hand him the key to the mystery and say, "Go get 'em, tiger?"

Uh-huh, sure. Again the nagging question was back: Just what was she trying to do, hog the spotlight and leave the dreary clean-up work to Dino? One thing was certain: he'd never call her Nancy Drew again!

Nina finished drying her hair and began to dress. It wasn't as though she was going to take any foolish chances, either. And yet, she couldn't help remembering Scotty Lane's close brush with death, and the electrified desk. . . . Nina's assurance began to fade, but she resolutely ignored the slight thrill of fear.

Standing before her full-length mirror, she appraised her image from all angles. She'd decided on a scroll-patterned black and white silk dress that hugged her torso to the hips, then broke into a froth of ruffles several delectable inches above the knee.

A necklace of ebony and pearls and matching earrings completed her ensemble. The contrast between stark black and white and her flaming red-gold hair was dramatic and startling. Not bad for thirty-four, she had to admit. Pity Dino wouldn't be there to appreciate it.

The momentary apprehension over what the evening might bring was gone now. Nina tossed a short black cape over her shoulders, picked up her purse and left her apartment, locking the door carefully behind her. It was then 4:40 P.M. If she was going to be at Leatherwing by six o'clock, she'd better step on it.

Again, as she maneuvered her new sleek Mazda up the winding drive to the fabulous Meyer estate, Nina felt a coldness descend. As long as she lived, she'd never forget the dreadful things that had happened the last time she'd been here. Leatherwing—the name deriving from the vast horde of bats that nested in a collapsed barn on the furthermost reaches of the ninety-acre estate—was a well publicized showplace. It had been featured in New York newspapers, in *House and Garden*, and in many other such publications devoted to expensive real estate and cost-is-no-object interior decoration. Had Nina been writing such an article she'd certainly have entitled it: ''A Visit to Leatherwing—House of Horrors.''

The party was in full swing, with some fifty people deep into cocktails in the great living room when Nina arrived. She had barely entered and surrendered her wrap to a pretty attendant when Helen herself swept toward her, an overdone smile on her features. ''Nina,'' she purred, ''how nice of you to come. You look ravishing. And all alone. Why hasn't

173

some handsome Don Juan swept you off your feet by now? What a terrible waste."

"Thank you for asking me, Helen. And you look lovely, too. That shade of blue does wonderful things for your hair. I absolutely *love* those shoes." Behind the cordial facade, Nina wondered just what was going on here. Helen, who had so recently vowed to avenge herself on Nina for intruding in her personal life when her husband was murdered, acting like this? Not in character, not one little bit.

"Come in and meet everyone; Georgine and Sylvia have brought their husbands, most of the rest you know, I'm sure. Our guests of honor are in love with Leatherwing already." Helen hailed one of the roving waiters, dressed in a tuxedo instead of one of the period costumes she usually insisted on. "What will you have to drink?"

"Champagne, please," Nina told the man. "And, Helen . . ."

She turned to find that her hostess had fled and was already deep in conversation with David Gelber and Sally Burman, who stood to one side of the huge fieldstone fireplace in which a fire blazed cheerily. Carrying a Waterford goblet brimming with champagne, Nina began to circulate among the crowd.

As she discussed Scotty Lane's recovery with Noel Winston, Nina's eyes restlessly swept the gathering, her mind still pondering Helen Meyer's strangely warm welcome. Well, hatchets sometimes do get buried, she conceded. But with Helen she'd somehow expected it to land in her skull.

"Yes," she recaptured the thread of the conversation, "Scotty's looking much better, isn't he? I'm glad you went to see him, Noel. He must have been getting tired of only female company."

"Female company like you? Never. You haven't

174

noticed? Seventy-year-olds can come down with puppy love, too."

"Don't be silly, Noel. You're embarrassing me."

"I swear, he looks ten years younger. Nina, Nina, Nina, that's all he talks about. I suddenly get the feeling of being left out in the cold. And I thought I was your main geriatric admirer."

Nina caught sight of Sylvia Kastle, very chic in a black floor-length chiffon, accompanied by a dark-haired heavyset man who had to be Lance Kirby. He was obviously at ease in a tuxedo, a definite aura of influence and power mantling his six-foot figure. His eyes were hard and cold, never seeming to rest. A man who could definitely make trouble, she decided, when his penetrating gaze settled on her for a moment. Nina looked away. Did she really want to cross someone like this?

Earnest Claypool wasn't as threatening. He and Georgine were seated on one of the couches, chatting with Angela Dolan and Horst Krueger. With white hair and florid face, this shorter waddle-duck of a man was not at all comfortable in a black tie. Georgine was demure in a simple mid-length dress of burgundy-colored wool that helped overcome her mouseyness and projected a statement of quiet refinement.

Dinner was served at eight, and much to her chagrin, once inside the baronial dining room, Nina found herself seated to the left of Lance Kirby. Helen Meyer sat at the head of the table; the Claypools were directly across. "How do we rate?" she whispered to Rick Busacca, immediately on her left. "Up here with the royalty?"

"As far as you're concerned, Nina," he replied with an admiring glance, "it comes under the name of dressing the table."

"Flatterer," she quipped lightly.

It was obvious that the Kirbys weren't about to speak to her. Sylvia made no move to introduce her husband to Nina, and continued to stare stonily ahead. "Hello," Nina addressed the formidable man, forcing the issue. "I'm Nina McFall. And you must be Lance Kirby. So pleased to know you."

"Ms. McFall? How pleasant. Sylvia speaks of you so highly." And though he smiled politely, Nina could tell his heart wasn't really in it. She was sure Sylvia had mentioned her, but certainly not favorably. A similar effort with Georgine's husband brought almost identical results.

The space between Nina and the guests of honor could have been used to chill wine.

I'd certainly hate to be on the Kirby list, Nina concluded, her confidence quickly ebbing. It would be no difficult thing for building contractor Kirby to arrange for Nina to become part of the foundation at a current project.

Nina was grateful for Rick Busacca's trendy chatter. The cold shoulder she received from the Kirbys and the Claypools, the tiresome toasts Helen proposed to them, the cliché thanks for the contributions to *The Turning Seasons* (with veiled implication that the show was reborn, a Phoenix rising from the ashes) combined to leave Nina irritated, bored, and looking forward to the end of an endless dinner.

Afterward the guests again gathered in the living room for postprandial treats and drinks. Someone sat down at the nine-foot Steinway and thumped out a few show tunes, but it was almost ten by then, and energy levels were sagging. By 10:15 the first of the guests was in the process of leaving, which put Nina on edge because she still hadn't found her opportunity to confront Sylvia.

Some of the men had meandered into the adjoining recreation room, where they were taking in the

176

second half of the rerun of a Penn State football game. With some annoyance, Nina noted that Rafe Fallone was among them. But on the positive side, Claypool and Kirby were also seated before the TV. Nina set out to find Sylvia. A few minutes alone with the *grande dame* was all she needed.

Luck was with her, for she found Sylvia alone on a small couch at the far eastern end of the great room. But even as she squared her shoulders and headed toward her, Georgine floated into the picture, a cordial glass in hand, and sat down beside her. Nina hesitated momentarily, then reset her course again. All the better, she concluded. For the sake of appearances they couldn't possibly snub her again.

She drew up a large hassock, sat down right in front of the two, and pasted a perky smile on her face. "Well," she said, "what do you ladies think of Leatherwing?"

Sylvia managed a wintry smile. Georgine was a bit more open. "It's very nice," she said, "but so many rooms."

"And you, Sylvia?" Nina prodded. "Impressed?"

"Yes, of course," she replied grandly. "It lives up to its reputation in every way."

"Did you know that all our daily scripts are written on the premises?" Nina asked. When they admitted that they didn't, Nina launched into an animated account of Helen's insistence on the unique arrangement and shared a few anecdotes about the difficulties of the daily commute for the writers.

There was an awkward lapse in the conversation then, which Sylvia Kastle bridged in a most fortunate way. "I don't suppose you'll tell us, Nina, but I'm wondering if you've heard anything more about

May's murder. Are the police getting any closer to solving it?''

"How should I know?" Nina said, getting herself ready to spring her surprise.

"I happen to know that you're very closely involved, Nina. That you know more than you pretend," Sylvia stated coolly.

"Oh? And where did you hear a thing like that?"

"People talk. Especially on the set. Your personal alliance . . ." she put an unpleasant emphasis on the word "with the chief detective on the case is well known."

"And why do you suppose that this detective would share police information with me?" Any moment now . . .

Sylvia became wary all at once. "I can only make certain . . . assumptions. If you *are* seeing the man on the side . . . if you're . . . *intimate* with him . . ."

Nina stared hard at Kastle. "Oh? And how do you know about this so-called intimacy? You wouldn't have hired someone to follow me—and Lieutenant Rossi—around, would you?"

Sylvia flinched. "Of course not! How ridiculous of you to even imply such a thing. As I say, there's talk at the studio. Your relationship *is* suspect."

"Hardly as suspect as some of the things I'm thinking at this moment. Things like someone named Scotty Lane. Things like that little electrical *accident* I narrowly escaped on Monday. You wouldn't happen to know anything about *that*, would you, Sylvia? There's talk on the set about those items also."

"Sylvia," Georgine said hesitantly, "what is she talking about?"

Sylvia responded with a bit more force than was necessary. "Miss McFall is attempting a little subterfuge—a subterfuge that isn't working."

"Isn't it, Sylvia?" Nina accused. "You say I'm not telling you all I know about May's murder. Are you telling me everything *you* know?"

"Sylvia!" Georgine intervened. "Whatever is this all about? I'm confused. If I didn't know better I'd say that Nina is making an accusation. Is that what she's doing?"

"Nothing of the kind." Sylvia smiled stiffly. "She's simply blowing smoke. Trying to prove a conspiracy that doesn't exist."

"Conspiracy?" said Georgine, frowning. "I'm afraid I'm not following any of this."

Having achieved her first objective—to put Sylvia unmistakably on notice—almost as if a teleprompter was slowly turning just behind Sylvia's shoulder, Nina asked, "Tell me, Sylvia, did you have any trouble getting here? As I understand it, you live on Long Island, right?"

"Yes, that's right," Sylvia replied. "Georgine and I both do. What are you getting at?"

"I hope you didn't have difficulty finding this place," Nina said blandly. "How did you come?"

"No problems at all," Georgine offered, obviously perplexed at the abrupt flip-flop. "Helen supplied us with a good map. We all came out in our car. Earnest drove. My husband loves to drive."

Nina's pulse quickened as she approached her most crucial lines. "And when you leave tonight, will you both go back to Long Island?"

"Yes, of course," Georgine said, puzzled. "We live in Oyster Bay and Sylvia lives in Glen Cove. It's not much out of our way, really."

"I don't see where this is leading up to," Sylvia snapped.

"Don't you?" Nina inserted a three-beat pause. "I'm just wondering, Sylvia. Will the Claypools drop you and Lance off in Glen Cove tonight, or will you go to your Carson Place address? The apartment listed under Kirbonsyzk?"

Nina watched with intense concentration as the remark registered. Instantly Sylvia's eyes widened. Her jaw dropped almost imperceptibly. As quickly the eyes darted, looking everywhere but at Nina. Gotcha! Nina longed to shout. But she said nothing, merely continued to gaze at Sylvia, her smile fixed.

"Carson Place?" Georgine said. "What are you talking about? Sylvia, you never told me you and Lance kept a place in the city."

"Georgine," Sylvia said, her voice tinged with rage, "will you please be still!" Her eyes bored into Nina's. "How did you learn about that? No one's supposed to know that."

"A little bird." Nina raised a taunting eyebrow. She rose to her feet at that moment, staring down at a very stunned Sylvia Kastle. "You asked if I knew anything new about May Minton's murder?" she said mildly. "Now it's my turn to ask *you* again. But I won't. You see, I already know the answer. Good night, ladies."

When Nina emerged from the powder room ten minutes later, most of the guests were gone, including the Kirbys and the Claypools. It was 11:15 P.M. and the catering crews were cleaning up, clearing away dishes, napery and glassware. But Nina, on an adrenaline high, lingered on. Make it a clean sweep? she mused. Why not? All she had to do was follow up on the opening Helen had provided at the start of the evening.

Angela Dolan and Horst Krueger were standing in the entrance hall, their coats on, exchanging effusive farewells with their hostess. Finally closing the door on them, Helen sagged noticeably and headed for the bar, where she poured herself a brandy of staggering proportions. As she lifted it to

180

her lips, her eyes widened in surprise at finding Nina still there.

"Oh, Nina," she said, feigning a brightness her bleary eyes belied, "still here? Good. Why don't we have a nightcap together? I always hate it when a party's over and I'm all alone. Ever since Morty passed on . . . it all seems so grim, so final." She seemed on the verge of tears, and Nina suddenly felt sincere sympathy for her employer. Underneath the hardened producer there was really just a rather lonely widow. Taking advantage of her condition right now might be considered dirty pool, Nina thought. Then again, it might be highly instructive. Damn those ethical dilemmas, anyway.

"A Drambuie, very small," Nina said. Helen put a tiny gossamer-thin glass on the beautifully appointed bar and poured the amber liqueur carefully.

"It was a wonderful evening, Helen. I enjoyed it very much. Sylvia and Georgine were most impressed with Leatherwing."

"Really? I certainly hope so. Such wonderful women. I hope I still have that much ginger when I'm their age."

Ginger, Nina thought. Yes, that's Sylvia all right, gingery. With just a touch of curare.

"Helen." Nina pulled her bar stool closer to Helen's and peered directly into her eyes. "Do you want to help solve May's murder? Do you really want to know who killed her?"

"Well, yes. Of course I do. I adored her. Everyone did. But how can I help? I don't know anything." She seemed about to cry again. "She didn't deserve what . . . happened to her."

"You can, Helen," Nina said patiently, as if talking to an inattentive child. "You're probably the *only* one who knows. Nobody talked to her more than you did in the days just before she died."

"Me?" Helen said. Her attention captured, she sat more erectly on the high-backed stool. "Oh, I know what you're getting at. I talked to that detective friend of yours about the same thing. But I've already told him. I don't remember anything at all. Pour us another, will you?"

Helen was certainly making it easy for her, but Nina didn't think she'd be much use totally sloshed.

"No, that's enough, Helen. For both of us. Now listen to me. Let's go back, let's talk about those conversations you had with May."

"Not tonight," Helen protested weakly. "I'm so tired . . ."

"It had something to do with that murder that happened in nineteen seventy-two, when Tucker O'Brien was killed. The director who was her lover for a while."

Helen's eyes widened. "Her lover? She never told me *that*."

Patiently, Nina went back over the chaotic period when all three Glitter Girls had slept with Tucker O'Brien. Helen's eyes widened steadily. "No . . ." she said, "I never knew *anything* about that. She told me once about an old friend who'd been killed. But she never told me they were playing duets. And you say Sylvia and *Georgine*, too? What else do you know about this?"

"No, Helen. What else do *you* know? Think about everything May said to you when she told you about Tucker. Did she say anything at all about who might have done it?"

"No." Helen's head wobbled. "She didn't. She said, 'I'd give my right arm to know . . .' And then she said, 'I'm looking into it.' "

"*She did?*" Nina braced herself on the bar to keep her hands from shaking. "Tell me, Helen. Try to remember exactly what else she said. Take your time. Don't leave out a thing.''

''Oh, you mean about her hiring a writer to do a script? Is that what you're asking? I didn't put too much stock in that. She seemed to be trying to find out if I'd be interested in producing it.''

''A writer? What for? What script?''

''That show,'' Helen said irritatedly, as if it was now her turn to deal with a sleepy child, ''the TV special she was planning on doing.''

''Yes, yes,'' Nina urged. ''What about it? Oh, God, Helen, that's *it*! Don't let it slip away again. What TV special?''

''Is *that* what the detective was asking me about?'' Helen said irascibly. ''I could have told him that. All he had to do was ask.''

Nina wanted to scream with exasperation. She knew! All this time the woman knew. But nothing had jogged her memory because it wasn't important to Helen. But it was important—desperately important—to May's killer.

''Tell me, Helen. A special? What about?''

''Well, about the murder, of course. She was going to dig up all that old stuff all over again. Like Geraldo Rivera and that hotel of Al Capone's. She was going to tell who it was that really murdered her dear friend. But really, after all these years, how could she prove anything? And who cares? See why I didn't take her seriously?''

Nina expelled a long sigh. There it was. As simple as that. The motive for killing May Minton. Especially for whoever killed O'Brien so many years ago.

''That's the answer we wanted, all right,'' she said flatly. ''It's as simple as that. Helen, tell me this.''

''What?''

''I'm sure that Lieutenant Rossi must have asked

you these same questions. Why in heaven's name didn't you tell him what you just told me?''

Helen considered the question for a moment, but focused on a different issue. ''How could any woman think straight with a gorgeous hunk like that asking you questions? When he looks at you with those big gray eyes of his, when his face gets so serious . . . And those lips of his, so full, so sensuous. You just want to eat the guy up.''

Nina suppressed a grin. Poor Dino. So close, and yet so far. His sexual magnetism had gotten in the way. Oh Lord, she thought, wait until I tell Dino just why he missed the boat. And wait till I tell him about the TV special May Minton was planning! And—at long last—about the Kirbys' city address.

''Come on—one more anyway,'' Helen said, sliding off the stool a little too quickly and weaving her way around to the serving side of the bar.

''Not for me, Helen. I have to drive. Could I have a little coffee?''

''Sure, good idea. Pardon me if I don't join you, since I *don't* have to drive. I'll get someone to bring it right up.''

Helen fumbled behind the bar for one of the intercom phones that were sprinkled throughout the house, but she never found it. Instead, Nina heard bottles and glasses clinking together and Helen mumbling ''What in hell is this thing?''

Ten gallons of black coffee couldn't have snapped Nina to full alertness any more thoroughly than the object Helen had pulled out from under the bar and was peering at in such confusion.

It was the telescope. May Minton's ornate brass telescope.

Chapter Eighteen

Nina lost no time in extricating herself from Leatherwing. She managed to conceal her excitement at seeing the telescope and casually picked it up from the bar where Helen had left it. As Helen tilted her head back to drain the last of her fourth nightcap, Nina concealed it in the folds of her cape. She relished the thought of Dino's reaction when she would crown her story of the Kirbonsyzk apartment by presenting him with the murder weapon!

The Leatherwing parking area was deserted except for one old Mercedes, a leftover from Byron Meyer's collection of expensive toys, Nina assumed. It was just past midnight when she climbed into her pewter-gray Mazda and turned the key in the ignition. The excitement of her discovery suddenly wore off and she became keenly aware of her extreme vulnerability.

She checked to be sure all her car doors were locked and let the motor warm up while she collected her thoughts.

First, Sylvia Kastle had looked guilty as sin when confronted with Nina's knowledge of her secret hideaway at Carson Place. Then the murder weapon had appeared unexpectedly from behind Helen

Meyer's bar. Who had put it there, and when? Those were two questions Nina thought she might be well advised to let Dino handle.

But something equally as tantalizing was nagging at her mind just then—*why* was it put there? Not to get rid of it, certainly. Even if someone had suddenly panicked, there were dozens of better places to get rid of a piece of evidence, even so solid a piece as a brass telescope. To throw suspicion on Helen Meyer? Nina dismissed that possibility immediately; Helen's mystification at finding the object was obviously genuine. To muddy the waters for a while? Possibly. But for how long, and for what purpose?

Before buckling her seat belt, Nina reached over into the well on the passenger side and retrieved a pair of scuffed black flats she kept there for long drives. Three-inch heels, accelerators, and brake pedals didn't mix very well.

As she drew over her seat belt and fastened it, she thought about Helen, about the incredible ease with which she'd pried the elusive, so-vital clue from her. Of course, a small ocean of brandy had helped things along, Nina realized, and again felt regret that her relationship with Helen was still in tatters. But that would have to wait. She'd promised to call Rossi the minute she got home no matter what the hour to reassure him that Leatherwing had not again been her nemesis. She was late as it was; she didn't want him worrying any longer than was necessary.

Nina goosed the engine to steady, and her pulse surged wildly at the recollection of what happened the last time she drove away from Leatherwing alone at night. Holding her emotions in tight control, she carefully backed up, turned the car around, and began easing down the winding drive to the trunk road that led to the main artery to the city. There were fifteen or so miles of the narrow, twisting, two-lane

186

road, much of it skirting the high bluffs that flanked the Hudson River. In places there were drops of sixty to eighty feet.

Gradually her jitters faded. The road was completely deserted at this time of night, and she was reassured. The darkness, the silence, the steady hum of the finely-tuned engine provided a sense of security that lulled her. Down the homestretch, she mused. Once Rossi was apprised of the information she'd gathered, once he and his crew bearded the Kirbys in their own den, charged Sylvia with murder one . . .

At that moment Nina suddenly came alert, cramping her wheel to the right and braking to avoid an oncoming car that suddenly swerved into view around a wide curve, coming at her at a breakneck pace. The auto's high beams nearly blinded her.

She resumed normal speed and sank back into her reflective mood, once again sifting and resifting the details of her conversations with Sylvia, Georgine, and Helen. It was a mile or so further along that she became aware of another car—or was it the same car she'd just passed?—coming up from behind, again at high speed. She slowed slightly, slid close to the shoulder to allow passing room. Goodness! He was really moving along, wasn't he? A prickle of suspicion skittered down her spine. Now he was slowing, reducing speed, moving in behind her. But if he was in such a hurry, why wasn't he moving out to pass?

Oh, God, she thought, this is all I need. She depressed the accelerator firmly, causing the high-performance Mazda to move out smartly.

The driver was deliberately tailgating her, the headlights reflecting painfully back into her eyes from the rearview mirror. She was nearly blinded.

Nina reached up and flicked the mirror onto night-glare, keeping her eyes glued to the road.

Her speed was up to sixty again. If she slowed down, she'd be rear-ended. Did she dare to go faster? The road became more tortuous with every mile.

A phosphorized sign warned of a sharp curve ahead. Reduce Speed To 40. She jammed the brakes in warning stabbings, hoped the driver behind would see her in time.

Apparently he did, because she navigated the curve safely, rocking only slightly in her seat, then jammed the accelerator hard, surging forward. But she made her move a millisecond too late, for just then the driver behind hit the gas and deliberately banged the Mazda's back bumper. Nina's head whipped back and forth as the sound of crunching steel boomed inside the car. Nina screamed and clung to the wheel with all her strength, fighting to keep her car on the road.

Oh, no! she wailed inwardly. My new car! It's not even three months old!

Then she was rammed again, even more savagely this time, the collision rocking the Mazda wildly. Someone was deliberately trying to run her off the road!

Wildly she searched the rearview mirror, trying to catch some glimpse of her tormentor, but her attempts were futile; the glaring headlights and the suffocating darkness blotted out everything.

Get out of here, dummy! she lashed out at herself. Move it! Now! Outrace him!

But once more her pursuer outthought her, and as she swerved left, the Mazda engine roaring, beginning to build speed, the other car swept alongside. In that brief second she strained to identify the car, to see who was driving it. Again the darkness frustrated her; she could make out nothing. The car was definitely a junker, a pale blue sedan of ancient vintage. Thoughts of the car that had run down Scotty Lane flashed through her mind. Could it be the same driver? A contracted hit man? The result of this evening's event?

But how had anyone arranged it so quickly? No, she reassessed, this wasn't the result of her recent visit to Leatherwing; this one had probably been on the drawing boards all week, ever since the failed electrocution.

Keeping her eyes on the corkscrew of road ahead, she fought to keep the Mazda on course as she came into yet another vicious curve. She clung to the wheel for dear life, her breath searing her throat, sure that she'd lose it, that the wildly yawing vehicle would hit the shoulder and be propelled into a tree at any moment.

The Mazda staggered again as the right end of the other car's front bumper slammed into its side. Twice more the demon vehicle banged the Mazda, flinging Nina back and forth in the seat, the fabric of the seat belt sawing into the side of her throat, momentarily cutting off her wind.

Terror convulsed her. She screamed nonstop within the close confines of the vehicle, the sound of her own cries compounding her panic. Twice she teetered on the shoulder, verged on careening into a deep ditch.

Then, suddenly, miraculously, the junk heap dropped slightly back, giving Nina her head. As it began to recede, she got a fleeting glimpse of the car. It could have been the car Scotty had described. Never mind, just get away from it!

She hit the gas, once more determined to break out and outdistance the older vehicle. But again her reaction time was flawed. This time the car skirted her rear end on the right side, giving the bumper on that corner a mighty whack. Then it dipped onto the shoulder and came at the virginal paneling on the passenger side. Instantly the Mazda was slingshotted left, across the center line, toward the opposite shoulder.

Nina realized with a nearly paralyzing terror that she was next to the steep bluff fronting the western bank of the Hudson. Only the thin, cabled guardrail and a narrow plateau of open rock stood between her and a sheer drop through open space to the rocks below. The hit man was hemming her in, deliberately herding her in that direction. He was moving in for the kill. One more ramming on the left side, and she'd go over.

Nina's screams turned into suffocating gasps. Her vision became blurry, and though she was aware of the approaching guardrail, she found it all but impossible to focus on it. *I'm going over!* the words shrieked, ricocheting on the inner walls of her skull. *I'm going to die!*

She heard another louder crash of metal on metal, followed by the building growl of the other car's engine. But she felt nothing; she seemed to be beyond sensation.

Fighting for her life, she was totally occupied in trying to bring the Mazda under control, to avoid hitting the guardrail and sailing across the bluff into open space. Everything else became a dizzying, background blur.

The Mazda hit the shoulder, bucked, and pulled to the right the slightest bit. She rocketed along a ditch and spun the wheel frantically, trying to bully her way back onto the highway. The car, seemingly possessed of life of its own, exploded from the ditch, veered, hit the guardrail and slid along the restraining cable, bouncing off one, two, three concrete standards. Then it came to a shuddering stop. Nina's car tipped at an extreme angle, the wheels pointed toward the road, headlights shining into the trees. Her head was flung forward, narrowly missing the windshield. Only the embrace of the seat belt had saved her.

She looked up in dazed surprise, just in time to see her battered pursuer whiz past, its engine a panicky bellow, its tires squealing. Only then did she realize why she hadn't felt that final sidesweeping.

The car's rear end was a mangled mass of metal, the rear bumper on the right side twisted high, the fender badly crushed.

As it screamed past her, she saw a third car—a newer, plain black model of current vintage, its right front bumper crumpled—in hot pursuit. She felt an unbearable surge of exultation. Thank God!

Nina turned her wheel hard to the right and gingerly restarted the engine. It caught raggedly at first, then evened out, finally emitted a feisty roaring of its own. She pushed the drive lever into low, slowly let the car have gas. It responded sluggishly, bucked, and died. She twisted the ignition key again, gave it more gas this time. Foot by shuddering foot, it moved forward, topped the edge of the road, then reached the asphalt.

Once on the pavement, the car seemed to shake itself like a dog that had survived a scrap. Nina felt the grinding protest of the twisted frame, heard the rattle of torn metal. One of the headlights shone straight up into the air. Amazingly, after the abuse it had just taken, the Mazda picked up speed. Vibrating badly, it began feeling its way down the highway in the direction the other cars had gone.

Minutes later Nina guided the mangled vehicle over an incline and saw in the distance twin sets of headlights and taillights as the two autos swerved on the winding stretch of road, the drivers moving

191

at breakneck pace. The lights blazed and dimmed as they braked in extreme turns, slewing from side to side. Up ahead, in a mile-long stretch of treeless terrain, Nina caught glimpse of the wide Hudson, reflecting the glitter of a waxing moon.

She coaxed more speed out of the Mazda and headed down the incline. She braked for the same turn that the other drivers had, then swept around a long loop that reopened on a wide panorama of the river. Even as she did, the other cars, half a mile ahead at least, picked up speed. She gasped as she saw the lead car swerve suddenly and lose control. The second car slammed on its brakes and skidded in an attempt to stop.

The puny guardrail went down like so many matchsticks as the lead car hit it at better than seventy miles per hour. She saw it tilt sideways the slightest bit as it cleared the cliff. Then it dropped like a ton of granite. There was one last feeble glitter of the taillights—the idiot was still leaning on his brakes—then everything went black. She imagined rather than heard the sound the vehicle made when it hit the rocks.

The surviving car was fishtailed halfway across the opening in the guardrail. As she cautiously neared it, Nina saw the door open and its driver step out. Her one good headlight outlined the man clearly.

Then she was scrambling out of her car, dazedly staggering toward him. "Dino," she cried. "Oh, Dino!"

He held her in his arms for a long time, until the savage shudders died down and her sobbing trailed off. "Are you okay?" he asked over and over. "Any cuts? Any broken bones?"

"I'm fine," she assured him. "Just shaken up. I'll be stiff, I know. But no real damage done. Darling,

darling," she choked. "Where did you come from? How did you know what was happening?"

"Didn't you see me? I passed you right after you left Leatherwing. I just needed to stop and turn around. I would have been there much sooner—I intended to wait in the parking lot for you—but I got a goddamned flat on the way. And somebody had made off with the jack. It took over an hour to get rolling again."

"But why? Why did you come after I specifically told you not to?"

"Nina, you've been acting really goofy lately. I knew something was up. I figured you were into your Nancy Drew games again. I thought I'd better protect my interests. Lucky thing I did."

"But who was trying to force me off the road? Where did he come from?"

"Must've been waiting on a side lane or something. He had his orders. He knew which car to look for. Only he didn't know you had a chaperone." Again he drew her close. "Dammit, Nina," he muttered in her ear, "when are you going to learn?"

"I've learned, Dino, I've learned. I promise," she whispered shakily.

They broke from a long, desperate kiss and went to survey the extent of the damage to her ravaged Mazda. "My poor car," she wailed. "That makes two in a row!"

"Mechanic's special," Dino grunted. "Bring your car in closer, out of the way," he ordered as he reached into the black car for a flashlight. "Wait for me here. I'm going to see if I can get down there and find out who's in that car."

He might as well have talked to himself. The minute she moved her car off the road, Nina ran after Rossi, following him doggedly down a trail that led to the base of the cliff.

They approached the car warily, with Rossi drawing his Smith-Wesson .357 magnum from a molded harness he wore on his left side. The only thing that moved was one slowly spinning tire. "Stay back, Nina," he said. "This won't be pretty."

Luckily the car had landed on the passenger side, so the driver's door was accessible. Rossi climbed up, managed to force it open. "He's dead," he announced flatly. He continued rummaging about, searching the man's body. And when he found his wallet, scanned his identification papers. "Genno Baratini," he announced. "Ring a bell?"

Nina shook her head. The name was slightly familiar but—"I'll have to see him."

"He's a mess. You'll be sick."

"I have to look," she said stubbornly.

Dino reached inside and pulled the man's upper torso from the wreckage. Propping the body with one knee, he shone the flashlight beam onto the swollen, bloody face.

Nina's stomach kicked hard. "Yes," she murmured, fighting nausea. "I've seen him before. He's Sylvia Kastle's chauffeur."

Dino patched through to headquarters on the squad car radio and gave precise instructions for the duty sergeant to send a wagon for the mangled remains of Genno Baratini. He gave further orders to dispatch a tow truck to bring in Nina's car. In addition, Rossi instructed him to find Charley Harper and have him wait at Barney's, an all-night diner near the intersection of the Long Island Expressway and the Cross Island Parkway.

They then collected Nina's things from her car and headed south toward the city. They covered most of the distance in silence, Dino driving with one arm and holding Nina close with the other. Each seemed to be gathering strength from the other's presence.

Nina was careful to keep the telescope wrapped in her cape; before beginning her story she had to sort out her thoughts, but they weren't as uncomplicated as she would have expected after identifying her pursuer. In view of this latest brush with disaster, Nina knew that Dino might react very negatively to news of still further deception on her part. She considered various ways to broach the subject.

Sweetheart, you might be interested to know that Sylvia Kastle and her husband secretly keep an apartment in . . . No.

Darling, now don't be angry, but . . . No, definitely not.

Honey, I was chatting with Helen Meyer a little while ago, and she told me . . . Yes! Yes, that would be a good opening, because it was information she'd only just learned, not held back from him like an idiot. Then the rest would come out naturally.

But she didn't have to break the silence. Dino did.

"Look, we'll be at your place in about ten minutes. I'm going to drop you off, make sure you're all locked in safe and sound, and then go find Sylvia Kastle and tell her she's going to need a new chauffeur. It's a legitimate call. We might learn something.

Nina wanted to offer to go along, but she knew it would be useless.

"So it was Sylvia after all," she said. He only grunted. "At least it was Sylvia's chauffeur."

"Oh, I think we'll find out she sent him. And he must have been responsible for Scotty Lane's accident and that photograph you received. Also the booby-trapped desk."

"Dino, you're not sure, are you? What's bothering you?"

"I don't know. From this point of view, sending her chauffeur to finish you off seems like such a *clumsy* thing to do."

"Yes. It does, doesn't it?" And so obvious. "Dino, how are we going to prove it was Sylvia?"

"Haven't you had enough?" His voice took on that back-off edge she was coming to know so well. *"We*, meaning you and I, aren't going to prove anything. *We*, meaning the New York City Police Department, will take care of the rest."

"Only asking, sweetie. But what do you really have? Sylvia can easily claim Genno was acting on his own, and how can we—I mean how can *you*—prove otherwise?"

No response.

Before Dino left Nina's apartment, they arranged to meet late the next afternoon; the earlier-planned meeting now seemed impractical. By the time Dino made the round trip to and from the Kastle/Kirby home in Glen Cove, it would probably be 4:00 A.M.

But before Nina turned out her bedside lamp, she had covered several pages of a large yellow writing tablet with closely scrawled lines of dialogue. Tomorrow morning she'd give Sally Burman a call and persuade her to help boost the cast's sagging spirits by joining Nina in a little skit. It would be a lie; Nina was sure it was going to be one of the most stunning performances she'd ever deliver.

Chapter Nineteen

On Sunday Dino arrived at Nina's apartment shortly after 5:00 P.M. Relaxing with a drink in hand, he described the scene when he and Charley Harper had awakened the Kirbys in the middle of the night.

"All the lights were out, and Kirby threw a shit-fit when he opened the door and I identified myself. Then Sylvia came down the stairs like some grand duchess descending to meet the riffraff."

"Surprising she didn't stay up to get the news flashes from Genno," Nina said. But she wasn't surprised at all.

"I told them I had some bad news, that there'd been an accident involving their chauffeur."

"How did they react?"

"Sylvia seemed only mildly interested. Kirby went white."

Nina's ears perked up at that. "Kirby? Not Sylvia?"

"You got it. Turns out Kirby was worried about his Bentley, not his chauffeur. So then I dumped it on them. Told then Genno Baratini had been killed in an auto accident along the Hudson, a couple of miles south of the Meyer estate. And he wasn't driving a Bentley."

"What did Sylvia say then?" Nina asked eagerly.

"Something surprising. She said, "I never trusted that man for a moment. He was always asking for time off, and now we hear that he was sneaking around, spying on us. He was probably following the four of us in Georgine's car. It's a wonder we weren't *all* killed!"

He paused, and Nina raised a quizzical eyebrow at him.

"Nina, that didn't sound like a guilty conscience to me."

"Nor to me. Sounds like Sylvia being Sylvia."

"So then we asked them where to ship Genno's body and we left. There wasn't anything else to do."

Now start slowly, Nina told herself.

"Dino, I have a . . . an idea that—"

"No, you don't have an idea, you have what you were about to say. You have a *hunch*, don't you?"

Easy, easy, now. "What are you, clairvoyant as well as devilishly, irresistibly handsome?" His stony stare put an abrupt end to the cute approach.

"All right, call it what you will, I *believe* that one way or another, things are about to come to a head."

"Well, I hope to Christ you're right!"

"Dino," she murmured seductively, "let's give ourselves a mini-vacation. Just for the rest of the evening, let's not even mention this case or anyone in it. Let's just concentrate on us. I'll concentrate on you, and you concentrate on . . ."

There was no need to finish the sentence. There was no way, either, with his mouth pressed so hungrily against hers.

Later, instead of going out for dinner, Nina prepared a simple omelette and a tossed green salad. Then they concentrated some more.

* * *

On Monday morning, nearly everyone showed up for rehearsal a bit earlier than usual. There was an air of tense expectation that everyone seemed to share. Voices were subdued, there was no horse-play, and Angela even failed to deliver her usual morning thrust at Nina. Sylvia and Georgine greeted the group briefly and vanished into their dressing rooms until called for. Helen and Horst were there by 8:00 A.M. and stayed with the cast in the main rehearsal hall instead of going to their offices, which resulted in raised eyebrows all over the room. Nina thought the group seemed to be huddling together. For warmth? For protection? Possibly for reassurance?

The line rehearsal was uneventful and uninspired. Even Georgine's constantly surprising and entertaining line readings failed to provoke much reaction.

The moment Spence declared a ten-minute break, Sally Burman called across the room, "Nina! The new show is going to be wonderful! And you were right—such roles to be cast!"

A statement like that was bound to get attention in a roomful of actors, even if half of them were anesthetized and the other half were dead. The rising swell of coffee-break chatter died to near inaudibility as each member of the cast strained to hear what Sally and Nina had to say.

"Did it develop into ninety minutes?"

"Forget that—I couldn't keep it under two hours!"

Robin's curiosity was uncontrollable, and she blurted out the question everyone wanted to ask: "What show is this, Sally?"

Sally turned her attention to Robin. "Well, it had to be kept hush-hush up to now, but I guess it's all right to talk about it, since I finished the script." She paused, then uttered a statement that changed several lives forever. "Just a short while before she died, May Minton hired me to do a script for a TV special about the Tucker O'Brien murder."

There was total silence for a moment.

"And you finished it, Sally? Even though May was dead?" Nina asked.

"It was sort of a point of honor," Sally explained. "She insisted on paying me in full as soon as I showed her an outline, and then after she died I still had all that sensational background information and the research material she gave me. . . . I just felt I owed her something."

Noel Winston found his voice. "How did it turn out, Sally?"

"Noel, it's going to be sensational. The material is all factual, but it's going to play like gangbusters."

"Sally, dear," Sylvia interjected. "If the material is all factual, aren't you going to need permission from a lot of people who're still alive, not to mention the estates of some of those who aren't?"

Good point, Sylvia, Nina thought. You're thinking fast.

"May's attorney is taking care of all that. He says it won't be a problem. After all, the only one who wouldn't want to give permission is the person who shot Tucker O'Brien. All the others would want their names cleared. Don't you think?"

Sylvia looked pained at the response. "I suppose you're right."

"And wait'll you hear who May chose to play her own role—Nina!"

That caused a sensation. When the babble quieted down, Nina could be heard, still protesting that no, she couldn't do it, and Sally had to be kidding, and

200

why her, and where would she find the time, no less the nerve, to play the part of May Minton?''

''Cut the modesty act, Nina. You know you'd be terrific. In those years May was a riot, and everybody here knows what you can do with a couple of funny lines. Come on, just look at this, for example. Here—take this speech and read it.''

To the encouragement of almost everyone present, Sally whipped open the envelope and handed Nina a few pages of dialogue—the dialogue Nina had written the night before, now neatly typed.

''Sally, what do you expect me to do, audition right here?''

''This is ludicrous,'' Sylvia objected angrily, and Georgine, sitting next to her, murmured agreement, but their voices were lost in the general cries of encouragement.

''I don't know what the hell's going on here,'' Spence Sprague muttered to Horst Krueger, ''but this is the first time today this bunch has come to life. Maybe now we'll get a performance out of them. Let's just let this go on for a few minutes more.''

Nina was standing by this time, muttering to herself while she scanned Sally's pages as though she'd never seen the lines before.

''Sally, this is wild! I love it!'' And with that, Nina went into a devastating imitation of the performance May Minton had given so many years earlier in the movie she'd found on television late one night. She had the group screaming with laughter as she bounced from one actor to the next, at first following the prepared dialogue and then abandoning it and improvising.

''Now use a prop, any prop,'' Sally called. ''You know how May loved to use props.''

''Okay, how's this?'' Nina grabbed an empty coffee mug and pretended to break it over Rafe Fallone's head, which elicited good-natured applause from Robin Tally and laughter from the others. Next, she picked up a wastebasket and froze in mid-gesture.

"I'm stuck!" she said. "Sylvia, what would May do with a wastebasket? Give me some help!"

"May Minton never used any such ridiculous prop," Sylvia icily responded.

"Okay, so don't help me out! Come on, Georgine, you'd know!" Georgine, motionless, merely stared at Nina's spontaneous but eerily accurate recreation of the young May Minton.

"Or this!" Suddenly Nina was holding the brass telescope, pointing it directly at the two women. The expression on her face was enigmatic, and the group fell silent. Whatever the game was, the rules had abruptly changed. "This is the kind of prop May used all the time. What did she do with it? Look through it? Point with it? Bash somebody over the head with it? How did she hold it? How would *you* hold it? Show me!" With that, Nina tossed the telescope at Sylvia and Georgine and turned her back to them, breathing hard but not moving a muscle.

Without warning, Georgine Dyer leaped from her chair and grabbed the descending instrument. Continuing the same movement, she raised it over Nina's head as the others watched, frozen in surprise. Dino rushed out from the spot where he and Charley Harper had been concealed since 7:00 A.M., long before Nina had arrived. Shoving people right and left, he pushed through the group.

But he was too late. The glittering instrument crashed down onto Nina's skull.

And shattered into several pieces.

"You couldn't let it alone, could you? You couldn't let it alone!" Georgine's voice rose to a hysterical shriek as Dino restrained her. Then she collapsed and the room broke into an uproar.

In the ensuing confusion, Nina knelt down and whispered to Georgine, "Why did you kill May? Why?"

Georgine looked at Nina without seeing her. "Why not? What else could I do?"

"Is that a confession?" Nina asked Dino.

"It'll do for now," he said, as Charley Harper led Georgine away. Then he turned to Nina and held her in his gaze for an uncomfortably long time. "You did it again, didn't you?" he said wearily. "You did it again."

Nina wasn't sure how to take the remark, but there was no time to respond. At that moment a hand reached out and whipped her around so fast her neck ached.

"*You did it again!*" Helen Meyer screamed at her, unintentionally repeating Dino's words, but with unmistakable meaning. "You did it again! Couldn't you have waited until the end of the week? We'd have been finished shooting her scenes by then! Now what are we going to do?" Helen turned and addressed her ferocious plea to the entire group. "How the hell are we going to get this goddamned show taped today?"

There was a beat, and suddenly there were as many suggestions as there were people in the room. Which was entirely too many.

Horst Krueger stood on a chair and called for silence.

"All right, we're going to have to come up with something drastic. Again. Forget today's script. Without Georgine it's hopeless. We'll have a solution by tomorrow morning, and some new material. Sally seems to be on a creative kick these days. She's sure to come up with something fresh." He glared at Sally, who stood to one side, still awed at the result of her charade with Nina.

"Horst, don't blame Sally," Nina said. "This was all my doing."

He directed a particularly incredulous look at her.

"No! Not really? *Your* doing? Now who'd believe that???"

Nina ignored his sarcasm as she hurried from the room in search of Dino, who'd left unobserved when Helen began her tirade. Nina found him in her dressing room. He seemed to be in a thoughtful mood.

"Shut the door," he said quietly. "We have to talk."

Chapter Twenty

Nina hesitated in the doorway for a moment, caught between a rock (Dino) and a hard place (the rehearsal hall). She decided there wasn't much to choose between them and opted for the rock. At least here something might be gained. She closed the door and sat down.

For a moment neither of them spoke. Nina tried to read Dino's face, but he was impassively studying the tips of his shoes. Go very softly now, she told herself, and resisted the urge to reach out and gently touch his hand. At the moment there was nothing she wanted so badly as to touch him.

Finally he raised his eyes to hers. She thought it best to take the first step herself.

"Would you like me to just talk, or would you rather ask me questions?" she asked in a small voice.

"Does it matter? You'll do what you want to do in any case."

This was going to be worse than she thought. Skip the rule-playing formalities and jump right into it.

"Dino, I knew it couldn't be Sylvia. It was just too obvious, there were too many hints that she was guilty. Sylvia's not that dumb. If she wanted to murder someone—which I don't believe is in her—she wouldn't leave such an easy trail. I was certain somebody was trying to set her up. And then when—"

"An easy trail? I don't remember any easy trail. Or are you still salting away clues?"

Get it all out quickly, and let him erupt. "This is what happened . . ."

But he didn't erupt. As Nina related her discovery of the Kirbonsyzk apartment at Carson Place, the conversation with Helen after the dinner party, and the discovery of the telescope behind the bar at Leatherwing, he sat motionless, looking at her with a cold steadiness that she found unbearable.

"So I was heading home to call and tell you all this when that car began to ram into me. There wasn't time. Dino, when you stepped out of that car, I was never so glad to—"

"And then later, on the drive back to your place, and before I left you that night, and the next day, and the next evening? There still wasn't *time*?"

The single word tore out of his throat with so much pain Nina thought she might cry.

"Yes, there was time then. Dino, the reason I didn't say anything then was because I had a hunch . . ." Oh God, "had a hunch"? That would surely push him off the deep end! "You'd still believe Sylvia was guilty. There were so many indications that she was, and then the fact of the secret apartment had me half believing she'd done it. It was the kind of thing you place so much importance on, and you *should*, you really should, that's your business."

"Save the grease job!"

That hurt. Damn it, she was doing her best. "And *you* save the sarcasm! I'm trying to tell you things that I'm uncomfortable about, and it's not easy."

He considered her unexpectedly starchy come-back for a moment. "Go on."

"All right. When you pulled the driver's body out of the car and we saw who it was, that was when I knew Sylvia hadn't killed May." His eyebrows twitched in curiosity. "Sylvia's too smart to take a chance like that. She'd know Genno might fail, and then the trail would have to lead directly back to her. But if somebody *else* had sent Genno, there was no way to lose! If he succeeded, I'd be out of the way, and if he got caught, the finger would be point-ing at Sylvia. And I think that's exactly what Geor-gine wanted. She didn't care about getting rid of me, not really, although it nearly happened. She just wanted Sylvia to be found guilty of murdering May."

She paused briefly. Was he thawing out? Maybe just a little, around the edges. Press on, McFall.

"But the one thing Georgine *didn't* count on was that someone would appear out of nowhere and save me. She didn't count on you."

He shifted in his chair. What was that? Modesty? Appreciation?

"Continue." No, just a numb tail.

"So I decided to try to sort things out and set a trap. I didn't sleep late on Sunday. I called Sally Burman and told her I thought the cast would be really down on Monday morning and that I wanted to play a little joke to liven things up. Before going to sleep Saturday I'd written out a sort of little play, I said, and Sally agreed. So she came over and we rehearsed it a few times on Sunday. And then we gave our performance on Monday." She looked at him expectantly. Come on, darling, help me out, even a little. Please?

"You're too modest. That was only one of your performances. You'd already given a performance

207

for me in the car, hadn't you? All that cozy closeness while you kept the goddamn murder weapon hidden from me?''

"It would have implicated the wrong person!"

"And then your performance in your apartment, about how we couldn't get together early because you needed your sleep?" His volume was steady, but the intensity was growing. "And then your best performance of all, the one on Sunday evening!"

"That was *not* a performance! You know it wasn't."

"Let's stick to facts. You didn't know I was in the rehearsal room this morning. You might have gotten your head bashed in. You were taking a terrible chance with your life!"

"No I wasn't! I'd substituted the fake telescope for the real one. It was made of balsa wood. You couldn't kill a fly with it."

"Where did you get a fake telescope?"

"I borrowed it. From Sylvia."

"From *Sylvia*?"

"Where else could I get an identical fake telescope on such short notice? I *knew* she was innocent."

"You were still taking a stupid chance. Suppose Georgine had had a gun and tried to blow your head off instead of cave in your skull?"

"Well, she didn't. Now, as you said, let's stick to facts. Do you know *why* Georgine did all this?"

"No, I don't. But you probably have a hunch."

"No, not this time. You'd better find out for yourself."

He regarded her impersonally for a moment, then stood and moved toward the door.

"Dino?" He turned to her. "Will you let me know what happens?"

"Certainly. Your help on this case has been in-

208

valuable. You have the Department's sincere appreciation. You shouldn't have to read the rest in the newspapers."

"Thank you."

He seemed to want to say more, but limited himself to a curt, "You deserve better than that."

Dino left, closing the door quietly. She stared at it for a long time, then whispered to the empty room, "Thank you, Lieutenant. I think so, too."

Four days later, to mark the end of the most difficult week ever seen at TTS, Nina invited a carefully selected group to dinner at her favorite restaurant, Zenobia's. She presided over a table at which sat Sylvia Kastle, Angela Dolan, Mary Kennerly, Noel Winston, and her guest of honor, Scotty Lane.

The three older women had become particularly chummy due to the solution to the script dilemma devised by Helen, Horst, and the writers: Angela would continue to perform the functions originally intended for May Minton, and Georgine's role would be transferred to Mary Kennerly. Sylvia, of course, would continue to be Sylvia. Mary's first scenes with the new comic material were highly successful, and Nina suspected the white-haired actress would at last come into her own as a name performer.

They settled in at the table and raised their glasses in unison as the waiter finished pouring the first of many bottles of champagne—with a special pitcher of orange juice for Sylvia's beloved mimosas.

"To Nina," Sylvia offered, "without whom I don't want to think about it."

"No—to Scotty Lane," Nina said. "My source of all things true and reliable."

"No, to Noel Winston," Scotty said, picking up

209

his cue neatly. "Because he introduced me to my favorite redhead."

"No, to hell with all that," Mary said. "Let's drink!"

The full story had appeared in the papers only that morning, after the police completed their investigation and Dino Rossi had held a press conference.

The accounts detailed how Georgine Dyer had slowly been driven insane as the result of years of resentment toward both May and Sylvia. Professionally, she always hated being the low man on the totem pole, receiving the smaller, less flashy roles while May always starred. And privately, she blamed Sylvia when Tucker O'Brien ditched her. Inevitably, the table talk centered on the case.

"I want to know why May Minton left so much money to Noel," Mary Kennerly demanded.

Noel seemed embarrassed at the question, so Nina answered. "Guilty conscience, probably. Despite her reputation as a hell-raiser, she was basically a kind person, and what she did to people so many years ago must have bothered her."

"Did you really steal Tucker O'Brien from Georgine?" Mary asked Sylvia. Never one to beat around the bush, she was now a force to be reckoned with.

Sylvia raised a perfectly pencilled brow. "Are you joking, Mary? Nobody ever stole anyone from Tucker O'Brien. He dillied with one girl until he was ready to dally with the next. I knew he had his eye on May long before he gave me the Rolls. That was his kiss-off present, the big s.o.b."

"He must have handed out a lot of Rolls-Royces," Nina said.

"Oh, you got a Rolls only if your name was above the title of your last show or movie," Sylvia said. "Featured performers got Caddies. Waitresses and hat-check girls got Chevies. Most of the mourners at

210

Tucker's wake were girls who still hadn't gotten a car out of him.''

"No wonder Georgine's father shot him," Noel said. "But why didn't the police ever find that out?"

"Considering all the women in Tucker's past, there were probably too many outraged husbands and fathers and boyfriends to check on them all. And, as Georgine admitted, her father was some kind of a nut. Apparently he got crazier and crazier, and decided to do it many years after his baby was jilted. Then he disappeared. He must have just dumped the gun somewhere, and it was never found."

"Lucky for him he didn't shove it under Helen Meyer's bar," Angela said. "The dust never settles there."

"Why did Georgine stash the telescope there?" Mary asked. "And when?"

"It must have been easy to find a moment during Helen's dinner party," Nina answered. "And I think she did it simply to confuse the issue. She had to do something with it."

"Actually, Georgine didn't do that," Sylvia said sheepishly. All attention was immediately glued to her. "*I* did it." She hurried on, to avoid the inevitable barrage of questions. "Georgine must have hidden the damn thing in my apartment after she used it on May. When I found it, just before Helen's party, I was in a panic. It looked just like the copy May had given me, but I knew it was real because it weighed so much. So obviously somebody was trying to frame me. I jammed it into my purse— thank God it was so short when it was collapsed— and carried it to the party. I shoved it under the bar just before we went in to dinner. Do you suppose the police need to know that?"

"It wouldn't change anything, so why don't we

just keep that wrinkle to ourselves?'' Nina suggested.

"Nina, please! That's not a word one uses in present company,'' Angela said, astonishing everyone by showing signs of becoming a human being.

"You know,'' Sylvia said, "the part of all this that I find most insulting is that Georgine should be carrying on with *my* chauffeur! That's incredible. I always thought Genno was on the stupid side, but surely he could have done better than Georgine!''

"I think he was just being used,'' Nina speculated. "We know that he was doing her bidding all along. I mean, he's the one who tried to run down my wonderful Scotty.'' She was tickled to see Scotty's blush. "And he dropped off that threatening photograph, too.''

"Did he also wire the desk when you were nearly electrocuted?'' Mary asked.

"No—that was Georgine. She borrowed his uniform and passed herself off as one of the extras that day we shot all the background scenes. She must have picked up a lot of technical knowledge after retiring from the stage.''

"When she was learning how to work on film restoration,'' Scotty suggested.

"Exactly. And that also explains the videocassette of the outtakes that we found. Georgine prepared it from her own prints to highlight the fact that the famous telescope was missing and was probably the murder weapon. She must have put it there when she killed May, and then removed Sylvia's photograph from the wall and hid the telescope in Sylvia's apartment only a few floors away.''

"She probably found out about the apartment and got a key from that bastard, Genno,'' Sylvia said. "Lance always said if I told anyone about that apartment, it'd wind up costing him a fortune. I don't understand tax loopholes or any of that stuff, so I just kept my mouth shut about it. Nobody knew—well, Genno knew, of course. Actually, it was fun to have a secret hideaway, and go in and out with the security guards pretending they didn't see me.'' Nina looked dubious. ''After all, Lance *built* the damn place. He certainly had enough influence to arrange a simple little thing like that.''

''But that still doesn't explain how Georgine got past building security,'' Noel said. ''When she made the full confession, did she explain how she did it?''

''No, the newspapers didn't say anything about that,'' Nina responded.

''But don't *you* know?'' Sylvia asked, making an unspoken but clear reference to Nina's personal liaison with the police.

''Nope. All I know is what I read in the papers,'' Nina said. Which was regrettably true. She hadn't heard a word from Dino since the day he'd walked out of her dressing room.

Nina's dinner party ended only because Zenobia's closed at midnight. As a final treat, she had limousines waiting outside to whisk everyone to their homes. She rode in Angela's limo, stopping first to deliver her to her building.

''Nina, it's been a wonderful evening,'' Angela said, squeezing her hand warmly. ''And I want to say that even though we've had some bumpy times, I consider you one of the . . .''

''Don't, Angela. It's not necessary. I know, and I feel the same way. Despite everything that passed, I think you're a terrific person.''

''You are, too, Nina. Now let's cut this reconciliation scene short before the mascara starts to run.''

213

With a swift light peck on Nina's cheek, Angela was out of the car and into her building.

Who'd've thunk it? Chalk up another for the soft approach, Nina said to herself.

When she reached her building, she tipped the driver generously and rode up in the elevator to her apartment, anticipating a nice hot soak in the tub before climbing into bed.

But first she had to check the answering machine. How did actors get along before answering machines were invented?

The first two messages were from the studio, supplying details of the schedule for the week to come.

The third was from Dino. She froze as his voice rumbled out of the tiny speaker.

"Nina? Dino. It's Friday, ten to twelve. I'm coming over to your place. If you're not there, I'll wait. This is important."

Ten to twelve? Noon or midnight? Be factual, Lieutenant! If it was noon, he'd have come and gone by then, given up. No, he wouldn't do that in the morning, he knew her shooting schedule. Then it must be midnight. Ten to twelve was half an hour ago. That meant he was on the way, probably almost there. That meant . . .

The intercom buzzed.

"Hello?"

"Ms. McFall, you have a visitor. Mr. Rossi. Shall I send him up?"

"Yes, Willie. Send him up."

During the two minutes it took for Dino to reach her door, she brushed her hair, checked her makeup, applied a fresh dab of perfume, adjusted the lights in the living room, and tuned the radio to an easy-listening station.

But when the buzzer sounded, she reconsidered. "One minute!" she called through the door, and

214

ran around turning up the lights and snapping off the radio. When she opened the door, she found herself gazing into the same stolid expression Dino had worn during their most recent meeting, four days earlier.

"You owe me an explanation," she said by way of a greeting. It wasn't what he'd expected. "In fact, *two* explanations. No, three. Have a seat. First, I still don't know how Georgine got past security at Carson Place. Would you mind explaining that?"

"Easy. Same way she wired the desk."

"You mean she posed as Genno? That doesn't make sense."

"No. Remember, Georgine is a consummate actress. She found out that Lance had arranged for Sylvia to enter and leave Carson Place unchallenged, so she did the obvious thing."

"She posed as Sylvia?" Nina asked.

"Right."

"Why didn't we think of that?" Nina wondered aloud.

"Don't know."

"Okay, second question. What happened to May Minton's nephew? The guy from Maine who turned up absent."

"He turned up present two days ago. Went on a job-hunting junket up the coast. When he heard how much money May left him, he quit the job before he started and bought himself a new car, a new lobster boat, and a seafood restaurant in Bangor."

"Oh. Well, good for him."

"What's the third question?"

Nina paused, then murmured, "Where have you been all week?"

"I was sore, that's where I've been. What did you think?"

"I didn't know what to think."

"I'm still sore. You should have trusted me, Nina. What kind of a partnership is it when one partner doesn't trust the other partner?"

"Oh? Then tell me something else. How did you come to be hidden away there at the rehearsal last Monday morning? I didn't ask you to be there."

"I know you didn't. I just thought you might need me. I just had a hunch . . ."

"You had a *what*? A hunch?"

Long pause. "Yeah."

"It's all right, you can say it, it's not a dirty word."

"A hunch! I had a hunch! Okay?"

"Well, it's a start. Maybe you'll get another one sometime."

"You think so?"

"Practically guaranteed."

Dino glared at her. "Whoa, whoa —hold it. We need to get a few things straightened out. You want to continue this arrangement?"

She considered the question for a moment. "Do you?"

"I asked you first."

"That's right, you did. All right, yes. Do you?"

"On one condition."

"I don't like conditions."

"The condition is that we share *all* the facts *all* the time. No holding back, no little pet theories, none of that private stuff. We gotta share everything."

"All right, Dino. We share everything."

"That's right."

"Including hunches?"

" . . . Okay, including hunches."

They melted together and shared a long, intimate kiss.

When Nina could speak, she said, "Now I want you to wait right here. We're gong to put this to the test right now!'' She rushed into the bedroom and tore open the nightwear drawer of her bureau. Minutes later, she returned to the living room wearing the granny gown.

''What's that?''

''My new nightie. I bought it for our weekend in the woods, and I want you to share your feelings about it with me. No holding back.''

He began to grin. ''What do you want to know?''

''Is this the kind of nightgown you want to see on the woman you go to bed with?''

''Baby, it's more than that. It's the kind of nightgown I want to see on the woman I wake up with! Now come here.''

As she leaned toward him, he caught a glimpse of something sparkling at the unbuttoned neck of the granny gown. There, suspended on a golden chain deep within the curve of her breasts, was the miniature detective's shield he'd given her months ago. Its duplicates dangled from her ears, glittering from between the strands of bewitching red hair that played over her neck and shoulders.

''Are you bucking for a promotion, or what?''

''What.''

The sharing continued, and nobody held back anything.

In Book Three of Eileen Fulton's Take One for Murder . . .

As a publicity gimmick, Helen Meyer has conducted a nationwide talent search for an actress to play a new and major role on *The Turning Seasons*. The contest has been won by Terri Triano, a feisty young woman as tough as she is talented. Nina McFall takes it upon herself to show the newcomer the ropes, and also to console Millicent Maguire, the first runner-up, during her brief stay in New York City.

Then, during a gala banquet at Tavern on the Green, Terri is mysteriously murdered. Suspicion immediately falls on Millicent, who stands to inherit Terri's juicy role, but Nina doesn't buy it—Terri, she knows, had a lot of enemies. In addition, Nina suspects hanky-panky between Terri and the show's handsome new assistant director, Rob Bryant, an irresistible Don Juan with whom Helen Meyer is having a supposedly secret affair. Could Helen's jealousy of the younger woman have driven her to commit murder?

While Dino Rossi and his squad pursue a more orthodox line of investigation, Nina can't help snooping around. Between them, she and Dino zero in on the killer—but not before the murderer strikes again, and almost adds Nina to a growing list of victims. . . .